The Oracle of Devor

A Novel

Monica McDowell

EARTH WORDS PRESS

THE ORACLE OF DEVOR. Copyright © 2020 by Monica McDowell, MDiv

Publisher's Cataloging-In-Publication Data
provided by Five Rainbows Cataloging Services

Names: McDowell, Monica, author.
Title: The Oracle of Devor / Monica McDowell, MDiv.
Description: Seattle : Earth Words Press, 2020.
Identifiers: LCCN 2020911608 (print) | ISBN 978-0-578-71372-4 (paperback)
Subjects: LCSH: Oracles--Fiction. | Witches--Fiction. | Magic--Fiction. | Fantasy fiction. | Paranormal--Fiction. | BISAC: FICTION / Fantasy / Paranormal. | FICTION / Visionary & Metaphysical. | GSAFD: Fantasy fiction.
Classification: LCC PS3613.C46 O73 2020 (print) | LCC PS3613.C46 (ebook) | DDC 813/.6--dc23.

Library of Congress Control Number: **2020911608**

ISBN: **978-0-578-71372-4**

Cover Design by Lindsay Tiry of LT Arts at
www.ltartsdesign.com

Published by **Earth Words Press**
Seattle, Washington, USA
Send to 5022 NE 188th ST, 98155

Cover by

10 9 8 7 6 5 4 3 2 1

First Edition

Printed in the United States of America

Dedicated to my father, Jerry,
and my grandfathers, George and Lester,
who all love to play

Also by Monica McDowell

My Karma Ran Over My Dogma
You are Light
Confessions of a Mystic Soccer Mom
The Girl with a Gift

The Oracle of Devor

A Novel

Monica McDowell

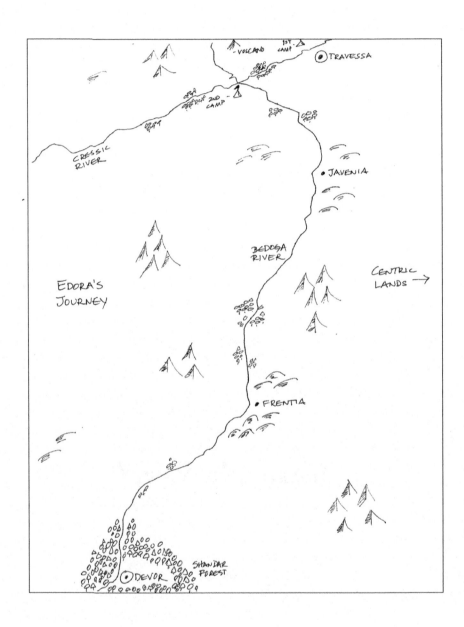

Prologue: The Vision

Ædora bent over the waters in the stone tower's courtyard—her looking glass. Picking up the birch wand, chiseled smooth by years of long use, polished to a sheen from the oils in her hand, she poked its tip into the still pool beneath her, stirring a wee bit just like her mamá taught her many years ago. As she whispered her chant to see beneath and within the ripples of time, the shadows of images began to emerge in the now frothy water.

She gasped. Never before had the looking glass deceived her. But how could this vision be? How could her scrying portend such a ghastly end? Why had this not been revealed to her before? The waters were as close to her as her own soul. Why would they betray her with such horrors?

Chapter One

The King, beside himself with grief, lamented: *What will I do without Niamá? What will become of this kingdom, my people?* He continued to weep in the bedchamber alone. No one would see him in this frail mindset, but he was undone to his core. The old woman lying on the bed was dying—his Niamá. She had raised him from infancy. When his own mother was too preoccupied with ruling and wielding her power, Niamá had been his true mother. When his queen mother had died, leaving him an entire kingdom to govern when he was a mere seventeen years of age, it was Niamá who was there for him then, too. He gradually became aware, though no one else was privy to her unusual abilities, that she had access to supernal guidance. Her advice had seemed to give him wisdom beyond his years, and it was indeed beyond him. He felt helpless ruling without her. She had stopped being his nursemaid, stopped being his substitute mother—she had become his oracle.

The fire in the bedchamber's fireplace crackled as with each breath Niamá labored heavier than she had before. The death rattle was near, he knew. He remembered it vividly from his father's last breaths. He had been only nine years old when his father, the former King of Devor, died. His father's death rattle haunted him still, in the dead of nights when sleep was the enemy. The foreboding sound chased him into narrow corners where fear overtook him and woke him from his fevered dreams. The King did not fear death itself. But he feared the empty loss the rattle foretold—the aching chasm inside that would never again be filled with the loved one's voice, presence, life. He especially dreaded Niamá's death. He did not want to face the possible catastrophes that could befall him and his beloved Devor without the oracle to guide his every step. He was still only twenty-seven—a young lad compared to the rulers in neighboring realms.

What am I doing? I am dwelling in my own misery. I am King after all. I can rule. I have been ruling all along. And some strength returned to his soul. But it was fleeting, ephemeral. Like a ghost of power resided in his chest, ready to evaporate into mist upon his first major decision without his oracle. He wandered over to the dress-chamber. Upon it, a porcelain-white, wash basin. Plain. Common. Non-royal. He splashed his face with a handful of water. He looked up. What was that? He'd heard a voice. It couldn't be Niamá, could it?

But after turning to look at her wan, wrinkled, beloved face, he heard it again and he could clearly see his Niamá mouthing words. He ran to her bedside, picked up her icy hand and said, "Niamá, shhh. You are spending too much lifeforce trying to talk. Just rest. You will be at peace soon."

"No, no." Niamá's voice was raspy, strained, yet forceful. Her spirit strong, even in her dying. "I must. I must tell you."

"What? What is it?" the King was anxious to calm her, yet desperate to know anything she could convey. Deathbed oracles were coveted for their accuracy and power.

"You will not need me, my son. You will have peace in your kingdom…" Niamá coughed and struggled as she choked and couldn't swallow.

"Be at rest, my dear Niamá. Do not worry. If we will have peace, I have no need to see you struggle so for any last words. Go to the Devorah. The mother spirits will keep you."

"NO. No. You will have peace for six years. Then…" She gasped for breath. She gasped again.

The King didn't want to hear what was next. Would there be war? Famine? Drought?

"Threats will come from the north. You will be surrounded. But another will come. Like me." Niamá's halting voice faded. Her eyes closed. Her breath shallow.

"Yes? Who? Niamá, you must tell me who!" Now he was frantic for the final prophesy. The King tried stirring her gently, but she had returned to her silence. He waited impatiently. His eyes wandered, flitting from object to object, trying to find focus, rest. The sun began to sink beyond the horizon, but he refused to leave her side. Out her bedchamber window, there was an eruption of color as the sun burst from fiery flame into the ash of night, preparing to rise like the phoenix on the morrow.

Turning back to her, he squeezed her hand, feeling little pulse and the chill of the grave. This must be the end. But who? Who would come? How would he know her? Niamá's breathing grew louder and her shoulders struggled as she sucked in oxygen through narrowing passages. Reopening her clouded eyes, she looked straight into the King's. With one tortured word at a time, she stared at him. "She. Better. Roses. Pauper. Six. Years. Remember. Son. You. My. Son. Beon. Keep. Her. Hidden. Close." He nodded understanding and upon seeing this, with her last word still in the air—the final sibilant still hissing—she breathed a great heaving sigh. Her chest rattled and lifted. Her pulse stopped. And all was quiet.

The King stood in shock of the death. The air whispered around him, like her spirit was still in the room, wanting to speak further. He did not wish it. He did not want to hear from the dead. He closed her eyelids, said a silent prayer over her body, wiped his eyes in grief of her for the last time, and left her bedchamber, quietly closing the door behind him. Why disturb the dead with loud noises in this time of heart-rending sorrow? As he trudged down the stairs to notify the royal medichè of her passing, he looked at the ancestral portraits lining the stairwell. They were depending on him. Their mantle was completely on him now. He could depend no more on his Niamá. Six years another would come. A lot could happen in six years. He put it out of his mind and after speaking with the medichè, he retired to his own bedchamber for the eve of the new phase of his rule. The new moon hanging in the darkening sky foretold its own oracle.

Chapter Two

The oracle was beside herself with anguish, pacing up and down the corridors of her chamber. She lived like a recluse at the top of a towering spire in the massive, grey, stone castle. The only tower that was taller was privileged to the King's access and his alone. Her own chamber took up the entire upper floor of the penultimate tower with access to a roofed, windowed terrace that jutted out from the tower. She was kept behind closed doors and closed windows at all times. She didn't like it and she didn't hate it. She was secure and she was provided for. It was enough and more than she'd had her entire life, prior to becoming the King's oracle.

At the center of this terrace were the waters; a manmade pool put in at her request soon after she had moved into the tower eleven years ago. Below her were six other floors, that she believed were all empty, except for one. On the bottom floor existed another residence that matched hers exactly in dimension and design, and she knew exactly who lived there.

After seeing the horrors that had displayed themselves before her eyes in those waters, she had run into her chamber and picked up her most cherished divining tool. Before she notified the King, she wanted to have twofold confirmation of the impending doom she had seen. Rummaging through her dresser drawer, her fingers found the velvety pouch with the preserved owl bones poking from within it. They, just like the birch wand, had been her mamá's and her mamá's mother's before her, both oracles like her. The gift had been passed to her through their blood—the oracular tools had been passed along from mother to daughter at the maternal deathbed for generations.

After grabbing the pouch, she had stridden quickly across the hardened stone floor to the other side of the main living chamber, her leather-hide slippers slapping softly against the stone in her haste. As she stood over the wooden table she used for dining, thoughts hovered just below her conscious mind: No one knew her in this life. Not really. She lived alone. She dined alone. She divined alone. But she didn't mind the solitude—in fact, she relished her hermetic life. Only the King even knew she was an oracle. Maybe it was her fate that she would die alone. Then the gift would die with her. She sighed.

As she held the bag of bones aloft in her left hand, she waved her right hand in circles above the crimson pouch. She spoke the words aloud just as her mamá had taught her:

> "Be to me the wisdom of the owl.
> Be to me the spirit of the wing.
> Be the eye that divines the way.
> Be the messenger that reveals night and day."

She lowered the bag, loosened the tie at the top that kept it secure and spilled its contents slowly onto the center of the tabletop. She inhaled. *No, it cannot be.*

For the bones had displayed their message all too clearly. Taking the shape of crossbones above a square they could only be interpreted one way: death would befall the house. The images in the scrying waters only amplified this message. Death was on its way not only to the royals, but to many in the kingdom, maybe even herself. She couldn't delay any longer. She must alert the King immediately.

She lowered her iron bell out the same tower window through which the coppery sun was just now beginning to arise. Counting the number of windows the bell passed until she had reached the seventh floor below, she double and triple-checked her tally to be sure of the bell's placement and then tugged quickly on the rope that held it, causing the fist-sized bell to chime its tone. She rang the bell with three distinct peals and then left it hanging by tying the rope to the metal grasp on her window's stone sill. If the escort had needed to verify the rings, he had only to look out his own window and see the bell hanging there to know he had been summoned.

12

She returned to her dresser and rapidly began changing her clothes. Normally, she did not have to worry about her wear, for the King and she met only once a month. But today, she would see the King, and she would not let him see her as he once had seen her, as a pauper.

Chapter Three

Havorth pushed back the bedcovers piled high on his bed and stretched his arms above him. He had slept well, though alone. His lover was gone on a journey with an unknown return date, but he had slept as if his lover were beside him all night. In fact, he paused as he was sure he could still detect the sweet fragrance of his amour lingering in the air. Havorth dismissed it at once as the conjuring of his nightly fantasies. He rose to make his way into his day's tasks—the primary being as the King's scribe, and he ordered himself, his clothes, his hair, and his breakfast as he did every day. He was fastidious in detail, thus making an accurate scribe, and even better in memory, thus making an extraordinary scribe. He approached every tangible in his life with the same meticulousness.

Just as he was setting up his ink to begin the day's copies of the King's latest decree, he turned his head swiftly toward the window when he heard a bell chime. Seeing a bell hanging just out his window, he watched as it swung and chimed two more times, rapidly and distinctly. He sat in his chair, unable to move.

Why would Edora be chiming me now? he thought. *She rarely rings the bell. Actually, she never has*, his excellent memory reminded him. He knew, as did she, that the bell was strictly to be used only in emergencies. Usually she just sent down a scribbled note on her rope if she needed something. *Ah well, maybe she has fallen ill and wants me to call for some medicine.*

Without delay, he went to the cloak stand, pulled on his suede overcoat, grabbed his massive keyring, and began the slow ascent up the stairs. Why Edora was hidden behind so many locked and secretive doors was a mystery to him. Mysteries did not concern him, though, nor interest him for long. He was a man of tangibles. He unlocked the first door, then ascended to the second. Behind this door was a sentry. He knocked four times with a rap, pause, rap, rap, pause and final rap—the secret knock.

The sentry slid open the window nestled inside the door and looked at the short, balding man through its opening. "Hello, Havorth. Good morning to you. I haven't seen you up these stairs this early in a long time."

"Ever." Havorth muttered under his breath, annoyed at this sentry's attempt at a collegial conversation when he knew Havorth was far more educated than he.

The sentry continued, "The first question is: 'What flies in the south, dies in the north and runs to and fro from east to west?'"

"The Cressic River." Answered the diminutive man definitively.

The sentry opened the first lock as the scribe heard the clank of the mechanism slide open. Again, the sentry looked through the window. "You sure do know your riddles, Havorth. The second question is, 'What does every woman desire, every man spurn, and every child have?'"

Havorth sighed. These questions were always so beneath his reputation as scholar, but he prided himself in his wit. He came up with them after all.

"Innocence."

The second lock glided open and the sentry opened the door inward. "Good day to you Havorth. You'll be coming back down, soon?"

"I suspect. Lock the door again all the same."

The sentry did as he was told, and the scribe hurried up to the next door. Each door had a unique lock and key. Try to open the door with the wrong key and the mechanism would collapse, trapping the key within and trapping the keyholder from ascending or descending any further. The scribe quickly matched the appropriate key to the next two doors and again went to the next door and rapped a different secret knock. The next sentry did as the one before him, but asking four questions, opening a lock each time with the correct answer and the scribe ascended to the next door, unlocking its unique secrets with the last key. He then climbed three steps and was about to knock on the seventh door, Edora's door, when she flung it open, looking at him in a fury.

"Where have you been. I rang you a full half-hour ago!"

"I'm sure it has only been five minutes, Edora. I left right after you rang. It takes time to ascend all of the stairs, open all the locks, and answer all the ques…"

"Never mind your excuses," fumed Edora. "Take me to the King at once."

The scribe was non-plussed in her flaming presence. He calmly stated the rule, "Your impatience undoes you, my dear. You know very well that you are not to leave this tower. If you need to see the King, the King will come to you when he has the time."

"He has no time! You must make this exception. I have to see him without delay," she reached out to his shoulders, intending to shake them, but at the last second, thought better of it and pulled her hands back, wrapping herself in a hugging self-embrace.

Edora's face was whiter than the scribe had last remembered it. She looked mad, crazed, even delusional. Why should he break the rules for a woman who was clearly unhinged? Maybe she was sick after all and needed a doctor's visit. He never understood her ramblings, but this—this was unheard of. To demand to see the King? How impertinent.

"Edora, you must be out of your mind. I can no sooner take you to see the King, than I can take myself. There are protocols to be followed, especially for you. It is the King who commands that you stay in this tower, not I. I will not be the one to break the King's law because you deem yourself more elevated than the King's decree and thus elevated over the King himself."

"OOOHHHAWWRGH," Edora stomped away from the door and returned with even more intensity etched in her fair lines. She was beautiful but the scribe was enamored not of her. "Havorth, you must—you must!" She stopped and regained herself, still speaking rapidly: "Then make haste, great haste, and fetch the King to me at once. Do not stop. Do not give up until he says he will return."

"I have no idea what he is doing or where he is. I cannot interrupt him if he is in an important meeting or even still asleep in his private bedchamber."

Urgency was not working in her favor. The more urgent, the more recalcitrant the escort became. She needed to gather her focus. Calmly, slowly, breathing deeply, she spoke again: "I have never asked this of you. Never. I have never asked this of the King. You must compel him to come. He will listen to you Havorth. He respects you Havorth. You have his high esteem. Compel him to come at once!"

Disdain for the lady-in-white grew inwardly as he considered her request. She was right. The King esteemed him greatly. He knew she had used his pride to gain her way and he knew he would go. "I will do as you demand this once. I will not do so again. This is highly improper. Normally I would make a written request and wait for the King's reply. But today, I will garner my utmost esteem and use it to prevail that he sees you straight away. Go back within. I will retreat with the doors locked as ordered."

"Thank you, thank you, Havorth. You have my highest esteem as well. You always have. Please escort the King per his usual entrance. I will await your imminent return."

The scribe turned on his way, brow stitched with threads of consternation and matching scowl, as Edora closed her door behind him. Being the King's escort to Edora was a high honor, but it made him feel more like a glorified sentry than a scholar and scribe. He found it demeaning to lock and unlock doors with silly riddles he had to change on a revolving basis so no one could gain full access to the seven doors, not even the sentries that guarded two of them.

He made his way through each door and lock, bidding the first sentry a side-glance and a muffled grunt. He ignored entirely the second sentry's attempts to engage him in a riddle of his own and re-locking the last door on the first landing behind him, he made his way through the castle trying to be as quick and as dignified as he could with his undersized legs striding along the ancient castle halls.

Since his wife's untimely death fourteen years ago, the King had stopped taking his breakfast in the Great Room as all his ancestral rulers had before him. The echoes of his metal utensils against the pottered platters of food in the Great Room reverberated the emptiness in his own soul. He detested dining alone in that giant wooden, barren womb. The noon and evening meals he could tolerate there as they were generally business-oriented occasions and he ate with trusted advisors, visitors from other lands, and honored guests. But this morning as with every other morning over many years now, he sat in his quarters, at a small table he both ate the breakfast meal at and where he looked over the day's agendas and ledgers. He was comfortable here—undisturbed-—and it provided a familiar, warm, small security. He had just finished noshing a delicate sweet roll, his favorite of the royal chefs, when the door of his chamber sounded of an abrupt knock.

"Yes, you may enter," said the King unprepared for this interruption into his routine.

He watched as the royal butler opened the large wooden doors. Looking appropriately doleful and apologetic, the butler bowed once, "My liege, forgive the intrusion. The scribe, Havorth, has insisted he see you. I tried to entreat him to come back with an invitation from you or an official entreaty to you, but he demanded he see you at once. He is outside the larger hall. I at least could get him to stay there until I had spoken with you myself."

"What? Why does Havorth need to see me? Scribes don't need kings. Kings need scribes."

"Precisely, your highness. Precisely. I can persuade him not of his delusion. Shall I tell him to return when he has the proper entreaties, sir?"

In all the King's years with Havorth, he had never behaved so impetuously. Havorth was a strict by-the-rules kind of man, knowing the rules of engagement with royalty better than the King himself. What was Havorth so desired of?

The King sighed. The day had nothing at all to thrill his sense of either duty or pleasure. He may as well invite Havorth in for the mere entertainment of it.

"It's all right, my son. Invite him in this once. I trust Havorth would not disturb unless it was worth risking his head over it." The King would never have used such a deterrent, though other kings did. He knew Havorth thought less of him for his light treatment of infractions. However, though Havorth knew his King's weakness, Havorth's inner machinations for the survival of his own head would weigh that the King still had the right to his head. Havorth would not interrupt for a small matter.

The butler bowed low with a slight nod of acknowledgement and closed the door behind him as the scribe was his to fetch.

King Beon returned to a few more ledgers from his accounts. The kingdom was in good stead. Peace and prosperity had reigned for many years. The oracle had seen to that. The knock on the door again surprised him though he knew it was coming. "Enter!" he commanded and sat a little straighter to at least appear to Havorth stern and unforgiving of this lesser sin.

Havorth entered quickly but with all the anticipated demeanor of expecting to be thrown to the guillotine. "Oh, my dear leige, please forgive. I had no idea I would be disturbing your morning meal in your chambers. Please, my liege, I offer my deepest and most sincere apologies for this highly indecorous intrusion. You must know I mean you absolutely no disrespect, in fact, I expect to be chastised most severely…"

"Havorth, what have you come for?" interrupted the King when he'd had enough of the scribe's self-recrimination.

"Oh, my liege. It is not for myself that I have come. It is for the lady in the tower. She insists on seeing you immediately. Oh, I tried and tried to talk her out of her foolishness, but…"

"What? Havorth, what are you saying? That Edora is requesting my presence?" King Beon demanded.

"Well, that is what we settled for. She first demanded that I escort her here. Of course, I refused to disobey a direct order from your Highness. Yet she would not hear of any delay in sending me to you…"

"Havorth, please wait outside in the Great Hall. I will have you escort me to Edora in five minutes. I will just ready myself and meet you there. You may go. Thank you." And with that the King arose, waited for the sallow-faced scribe to retreat in humble position while walking backward through the door speechless, until the doorman had secured it.

The King's attendants changed his cloak for his official overcoat, his morning slippers for walking boots. Beon gathered some personal affects he knew the oracle would ask of him, and he made his way to the Great Hall, asking his personal entourage to stay behind.

Once again, the scribe had become the escort.

As they made their way through the castle, taking the most direct route to the tower and the lady who lived there, the King was walking quickly. Tall and long-legged, his pace kept the shorter scribe-escort running to keep up with him. Never had the scribe interrupted him and neither had the lady in the tower. He would waste no time if she demanded his presence. He knew of the rumors. When his wife and he were without an offspring, many had thought Edora was his consort to bring him a royal line. But no, he could never. Not while his wife lived. And now that his beloved

20

companion was gone, he thought no more of his line. There were kin of good ilk who could serve with good minds. Edora would help them, too, when he was gone.

He hated the fear that kept clutching at his heart where neither he nor any else could tear it away. As they made their way through the secret knocks, keys, and riddles to ascend to each new floor and door, and arrived at the sixth door, the King instructed Havorth, "I'll be back in fifteen minutes. You stay here and wait with this door locked between you and us."

The escort, still visibly stunned by the King's sudden departure from tradition, nodded and bowed silently to bid his King farewell. After the King had gone through the doorway, Havorth locked the sixth door, and stood in the stairwell, alone, bored, and thoroughly unhappy.

The King waited until he heard Havorth had locked the door. He did not take the three steps up to Edora's door. Instead, he pushed on the stone second from the right and seventh from the bottom of the stone wall on the opposite side of the sixth-floor landing. With a shove, the wall revolved and revealed a door behind it. King Beon made haste to unlock this door with a key only he had to a door only he and Edora knew about, and then climbed the last floor that ascended directly into the oracle's private living area.

Chapter Four

The wiry girl scuttled along behind her mother, dragging her feet in the dusty path. They were on their way to market to sell their meager wares of bread, greens, and lilies to the villagers.

The mother said, "Edora, hurry yourself, now. The earlier we arrive the greater chance we have to prosper in our sales. Hurry."

"I know, mamá, but I don't like the way the villagers look at us." She meant, look at *you*, but couldn't bring herself to say that to her beloved mamá. Her mamá, whiter than the lilies in their baskets, was an oracle, a seer. Some knew this, others suspected, and most kept their distance as if her whiteness meant she was a ghost. Edora, too, was fair; the villagers—warmly brown-skinned, like the color of the tea from the blossoms of their russlet trees. She and her mamá were refugees from the far side; another kingdom, another realm. They had fled when certain villagers had ransacked their house, intending to execute her mamá for her "gifts." Edora's papá had held off the attackers long enough for her mamá and her to escape, at the expense of her dear papá's life. She missed her old life, before they were on the run. Her mamá had oracled for a villager that death was upon the household and when the eldest son had died, she was blamed for setting a curse upon the family. She had not, of course. Her mamá was a gentle bird who only honestly foretold what the signs revealed. She would never curse anyone, let alone a child. But the household upon which this omen occurred was wealthy, and the father held a post in the castle. He had the influence to drive them out and he did.

They had fled with nothing except their clothes and her mamá's divining tools that she kept in a velvet pouch on a string around her neck. They begged along the way before coming to this prosperous village in a wealthy kingdom and finding a thatched, unused pony barn to sleep in. They eventually found the owners of the land and offered the trading of wares for this humble place of sleep. The

22

owners agreed and helped them refurbish the old barn as a livable place for humans. They lived like the paupers they were destined forever to be.

It was as they arrived at market on a bright and warm Sunday, that the next event that would forever alter Edora's world occurred. The day was spent in the shade of big leafed russlet trees that lined the market square. Edora had grown accustomed to the background noise of bartering. In punctured her awareness only when she heard her mamá start into a new round of negotiations. Her mamá was good at bartering—being an oracle, she could read the faces of those who were simply a waste of time to offer even a miniscule discount to, as well as the faces of those who were eager for her wares.

As the day wound down and the sun's rays starting to wave farewell, Edora's mamá sent her out into the dusty streets: "Take some of our coins we've profited with today and make us the best buys you can on some fish, produce, and soaps to supplement our stores."

"Yes, mamá." Edora left the shelter and began making her way around to the booths of those who delayed bagging up in the hopes of last-of-the-day sales. She was able to procure a week's worth of soaps and produce, with a bit of salted fish that would have to last.

As she wandered back to her mamá, a young man, clear-eyed and stiff in posture, stepped into her path. "Who are you? You do not come from here. You're very white."

How rude, Edora thought, and sidestepped the interruption.

The young bravura was not to be so easily outdone. He stepped again into her path as she hurried her step. "You did not answer me? Do you think you're better than me? I doubt that. You should answer. It will benefit you." He stared into her eyes, willing her to obey. He had taken a liking to this one and he would not be spurned.

"I owe you no introduction. We have not properly met, and I will not be chastised to benefit myself or any young gent in so rude a manner." She met his stare that turned to a fiery glare, his skin burnished from the rage simmering just beneath the surface. Again, she stepped around him and ran to her mamá's side without looking back.

The young man watched her go, following her at a distance. As the girl and her mamá packed their wares for their parting home, he followed them without their knowledge.

His anger at being spurned by this waif made him seethe with the burning of a flame that had begun many years ago. He waited in the shade of the trees until nightfall, then drew close to the barn under the cover of the dark. Drawing a flint of stone and powder, he lit the thatched roof and ran off into the distance, not even turning to see the destruction he had ignited.

PRESENT DAY

The King was at the doorstep of Edora's living space. It took a moment for Edora to notice the obvious. Her mind was spinning in the galaxies of impending doom, and although she saw him standing there, it did not register until he took a step into her room, not waiting for her to invite him in. His movement triggered her awareness like a snap of the fingers, and in a moment, she was out of her traumatic hypnosis. Edora approached him and knelt at his feet.

"My liege, I do so regret that I have summoned you in this manner. I would have come myself to *your* door if I had the freedom to do so. I must speak with you. Tell you. I…" Her voice caught in her throat. She did not know how to speak the words that demanded the use of her vocal cords. But the King, perhaps knowing deep in his own self what was coming saved her speech.

"Dear Edora, please stand. Do not worry about the manner. I know you would never have called urgently unless you had grave news. It is grave, I imagine?"

Edora nodded silently as she rose. Her eyes tearlessly communicated the grief that had wound chains around her heart, restricting her breath, her tongue, every feeling. She held out her hand to receive the King's personal affects. She knew what would be placed there: an embossed ring passed down from his father's kin, a metal coin from his mother's, and his own talisman, an eagle emblem crest carved in ebony.

She dared not look any deeper into the King's eyes for fear there would be no end to the horrors she might detect in the depths of the mirror reflected in those dark pools. Thus, she turned and walked straight to her divining table. Displayed there were the owl bones still in their foreboding formation and beside them she laid the King's affects. She moved her left hand over the affects in a spiraling circle, whispering under her breath the words of essence. Slowly, the affects levitated, spinning with her hand. She moved her hand in the direction of the owl bones as the affects moved with her. Then whispering again, their whirling slowed and gently, eerily, slowed to a stop. She blew on the affects which appeared to remove the spell of her hand's magnetism and they sunk directly over the bones. With a word of release the affects descended to reveal their truth overlaid on the bones' divination. It was a layering of readings her mamá had taught her.

King Beon watched from where he first stood when he entered the room. He had no way to know what anything meant even if he had stood right next to Edora, and not wanting to interfere, he felt it best to stay distant and let her do her work. It was a mystery to the King—comforting, though, that even in the midst of alarm that there were tools that could reveal secrets.

Edora looked at the placement of the ring, the crest and the coin. All were in peril. They had all alit inside the "house" of owl bones over which had fallen the omen of death.

"My King," said Edora hesitantly but strongly. "You and your house are in grave danger. I have seen things I do not want to repeat, and alas, I fear there is no time to divulge details. Your kingdom is soon to be attacked. I know not how. But raise the alarms. Call out your guard. Defend your castle. Death is coming."

"But why did you not see this before?" the King queried pointedly—not accusingly but more out of exasperation. Worried, he began pacing. "How can I call my troops to arms? They have seen no threat! I'll be seen as a fool if nothing comes of this."

"I am sure you will think of something. But you must act now. I implore you. Do not mistake me. I am sure it will be within hours." Edora was spent. She had told her truth to the one person who needed to hear it. She collapsed back on her tufted seat, her face in her hands, a futile attempt to cover her eyes from seeing any more horrors.

The King stopped his pacing. Now was the time for action, not discussion. He was a decisive ruler when necessary. He said to Edora: "I will take my leave. I have a plan." Beon walked over to her, retrieved his personal affects, wrote her a note with the quill on parchment sitting on the corner of her table, and turned and walked out the secret door he had entered.

When he was back on the other side of the revolving wall on the sixth-floor landing, he knocked seven times: rap-rap pause, rap-rap, pause, rap-rap-rap. The scribe having heard the King's secret knock, unlocked the sixth door from below and then they both retreated back to the first floor of the tower, where the King departed from the escort without one word or even one look at his scribe.

If the King had looked, he would have seen his scribe, eyes wide with shock, mien disturbed with disgust at how abruptly he'd been shaken off like unwanted mud from a boot. The scribe was after all a man mainly concerned with how he was or was not respected. Havorth uttered some bitter words under his breath as he made his way back to his home, the first floor of Edora's tower. He slammed his door behind him, and while puttering around his kitchen, thought of delicious ways to avenge his honor.

Chapter Five

Back in his wood-paneled quarters, appointed with tapestries of burgundy and emerald—the kingdom's colors, the King summoned his chief security officer.

Once the officer arrived, King Beon declared, "Please deliver this to the General at once," as he stamped his seal on the hot wax affixed on his orders. "Remain at his command post until he has carried out my orders and then be ready to return here. You are dismissed."

The officer, standing stiffly at attention, nodded imperceptibly at her orders, marched forward to receive the sealed parchment, stored it inside her medaled jacket, as her starched uniform responded in like to her crisp movements, and she bowed and removed herself from the King's den.

After watching the officer leave, the King rose from his desk and removed himself to his private chambers. He had cancelled lunch with his advisors but asked them to be available for an impromptu meeting mid-afternoon. He needed to sort through his thoughts so when the time for decisions and actions came, he would make them with clarity, forcefulness, and confidence. The oracle, Edora, had never been wrong. Never. He would trust her words of warning, but he would only take action as proven necessary by his military. So, the first order of business was to set in motion whatever steps were required to procure tangible evidence that Edora's foresight was truth. This was not for his convincing but for everyone else's.

Edora. She had arrived practically on the castle's doorstep in a time of great crisis. At a time of impending war. Surrounded by a neighboring enemy, Beon had been hastening through the streets in his carriage to command his army to attack, when he saw her for the first time. A pauper, whiter than anyone he had ever lain eyes on, carrying a flush of crimson red roses, offered to sell her flowers to anyone who took a double take at the odd sight of such contrasting color on the side of the road. She looked at him with eyes that still haunted him in nightmares that had him fear his power. As soon as he locked his eyes with hers, something no commoner in his kingdom would have dared to do, he flashbacked to his Niamá's deathbed oracle. Pauper. Roses. Time of great crisis.

Ordering the carriage, "Halt!," he jumped from the open door, without waiting for assistance or to explain, ran back to her position at the side of the deeply-rutted road, and thrust a direct query at her as fast as he would a rapier in a duel for the winning strike, "With what do I rule?"

Without blinking or looking away, Edora immediately responded with a chill that sent warnings of shivers down the King's spine, "I see a ring, a coin, and an eagle, but your rule is true only with eyes not your own."

Momentarily breathless, the command to strike still strategically placed on his tongue, he again questioned this pale oddity whose stare, though unnerving, nevertheless rang a familiar chime for his troubled heart: "From whence then shall peace arise?"

She averted her direct gaze to just above his right shoulder, and began speaking in a stream of words, oblivious to the gathering of the King's security ensemble around this spectacle. They stood ready to retrieve the King from this young woman's madness.

"The King is about to bring death to many by one word. It is unwise. Though those who surround are threatening, and though the King's advisors have assured him of the victory, this kingdom will be greatly weakened and ultimately defeated. The only way to peace is through negotiating for food trade with the enemy. He strikes not for power but for privilege to more fertile lands in a time of impending famine. Send out a messenger to guarantee food to the foe in peace, warning him that through war and battle, the bounty of food and fertile land will be destroyed."

His Niamá's deathbed oracle had been accurate. She, Edora, had given wise advice on the precipice of war. After hearing her oracle, King Beon had at once ordered a sentry mounted on steed with a blue flag for safe keep and had delivered the message to the opposing General. Within a day, negotiations had begun that averted the war, and brought a strong trade with the hostile neighbor. It was an uneasy alliance, but necessary, and the years hence had eased the tensions between their rival kingdoms.

After peace had been secured with this rival, the King called for his servants to find and bring the pauper of a girl to his court. At first, he consulted with her at his whim, calling her out from the streets where she sold her meager wares. Rumor started to grow that she was his mistress. Deciding it best to have her within his walls for safe keeping after he looked up the remaining part of the deathbed oracle by his Niamá that he had written in his memoirs—"Keep her hidden, close," he sent for her to live in the castle permanently.

He chose the tower she still resided in for its isolation. Perhaps the less seen, the less talked about. At first the rumors grew, but in time they decreased to an acceptable murmur, spoken only by those who occasionally glimpsed the white lady in the tower that had become her home. It was at Edora's request that she be secured with doors and riddles. This lot was divined to her, including the scribe who would serve as escort on occasion. The King decreed these things at her insistence to secure the secret of her oracles. Most of her supplies were lifted up in baskets through her window from the ground floor. Anything urgent had to go through the escort. Edora had been an excellent oracle, better, he hated to admit it, than his Niamá. However, Niamá had played her own maternal role for him that no one else could fulfill.

As the King paced inside his quarters, ruminating on the oracled doom, his General on the outskirts of the kingdom's walls, had just opened the sealed orders. After reading the King's directives, General Morlay told the security officer, "Wait here in the command center until I return. You are to remain here without divulging why you are here or when you will leave. Is this understood?"

The security officer nodded stiffly. The General motioned with his hand to some chairs on the side of the partitioned tent. The security officer moved in order to sit, and the General turned and strode out of the main entrance without looking to see the officer's sitting. The General, though perplexed by the King's command, was swift to carry out his duties.

He approached the sergeant of arms providing security at the entrance to the cove that protected the command center. "See to it that no one enters or leaves without my express permission." The sergeant nodded with a statutory assent, stood straighter, and stomped both his left foot and the long weapon in his left hand on the ground at the same time as customary to emphasize agreement to the command.

The General continued on to the stables, satisfied with his sharp and skilled army. Nevertheless, they were unused to war, untested, as peace had reigned for many years. What the King was up to, then, with this scouting drill was beyond him. If there were a real threat, his scouts would have already seen it days ago. Was the King just wanting to see if the General's leadership was in order? To see if the General was still as sharp as ever?

As he mounted his steed, the General knew this was more a test of him than the King. The King would not be overthrown. He was far too popular a figure. A General, however, could come and go. Nothing was certain. He was being tested. He was sure of it. He would not let the King see anything less than the best in this drill.

As he approached the closest of the outer encampments, he slowed his horse's gait, and then dismounted still in stride. The auburn horse strutted at the impertinence of his rider. The General ignored this attitude as it was what made him great in speed. As the General strode directly to the guard at the tent opening, he asked, "Where is the scout?"

"Inside, sir."

Entering, the General caused an uproar. "Sir, we were not expecting you, sir," rang out as the men and women uprighted themselves quickly yet awkwardly. The low table they had been gathered around tipped as feet and arms hit it, flinging food and drink all over the ground.

"Scout!" cried General Morlay.

The shorter, darkest-haired man second from the General's left, took a half-step forward—all he was allowed due to the table's awkward positioning—postured and straightened, "Sir!"

"What report is there of any unusual activities."

"None, sir. All is normal. Occasional travelers in small bands passing by."

"Excellent. We are commanded by the King for all scouts in the outer encampments to scour the outer boundaries, looking for anything unusual in activity. Send out a messenger to travel to these encampments immediately. The messenger will tell all scouts to gather all intelligence, keep it secret, then gather here in two hours' time. Is this understood?"

"Yes, sir!"

One of the other men stepped forward, around the table and faced the General. "I am the fastest rider. I will serve as messenger if you command."

"I do. Make haste."

The scout, looking less than tight shipped in demeanor, cleared his throat. "Sir, I have just returned from a scouting expedition less than one hour ago. I am doubtful I will have anything to report."

"Assume the worst. You are a soldier. Be gone. Now."

The scout ran forward out of the tent, not looking back, feeling scornful, shamed, and defiant.

The General watched as the scout mounted his ride as did the messenger, both galloping off into the grounds surrounding the great kingdom-city of Devor to circle the posts in search of activity of any kind. Morlay then made his way into a small, private tent next to the lookout tent, apart from his soldiers, where he decided to relax. He had two hours until he heard back. It would take that long for them to position and then travel back. The grounds that circled the kingdom-city's walls were wide and fertile but beyond them, stood a surrounding forest, hilly with many routes, crevasses, and rugged terrain. Sitting at a low table full of dried fruits and nuts, he popped a dried fig into his mouth, savoring its sweet tartness. He then reclined against the upright back of the low chair and fell into a light sleep with fitful dreams of war, created by fear of the King's unexpected and sudden call to action. He awoke abruptly when the commissioned scout returned in a rush.

"General! Sir!"

General Morlay stood at attention still blinking away the violent images.

"The scouts have all reported back. Each has nothing remarkable to report. Nothing out of the ordinary, sir, from each scout. However, together their reports might mean something more sinister."

"What? What are you saying?" General Morlay growled. He detested delays of any kind. "Report everything at once."

"Yes, sir. Each scout's report is normal, sir. The only thing that each of them note is a normal band of travelers along typical trade routes, pushing their wares. However, what is unusual is that all of the scouts are reporting bands of travelers. And all travelers are described as being dressed in similar cloaks. At this time of year in the chill of winter, this is an unusually high number of travelers."

The General grunted. The scout was right. He puffed out his chest, stood more firmly rooted into the ground and barked, "This could be nothing. However, we have received word of a threat. We are unsure if this is credible information, but we must act as if these travelers are an army in disguise. We must be at arms and ready for a full attack in one hour."

"Sir,"

"You have your orders. Go!"

The scout, for the third time that night, traversed his route to the top of the highest hill to signal the messenger and the other scouts and to carry word of immediate attack.

The General returned to his central command tent, pitched high and wide and dyed in the colors of the flag, burgundy and emerald green. He would send word to the King that an unusually high number of travelers were accounted for and that they were arming to be at the ready on high alert within the hour.

Whether these travelers were a threat or not would remain to be seen. He would not be caught off guard. He had a strategy in mind to not tip-off those who might be ready to attack. They would be the ones who would be surprised. They would be the ones who would be sorry for attacking without honor, without declaration—sneaking up for war.

The General's ire was kindled now—as bright as a bonfire at midnight; his protective instincts for his King and his people—strong. No one would attack them and not live to regret their actions.

Chapter Six

$\mathcal{A}$ beggar stood at the city gates. The soldier guarding them was not certain when the beggar had appeared. He was sure he had not seen him approach. He looked disdainfully at the clearly bedraggled man—the bottom dregs of society. He reminded the soldier of everything he was running away from by becoming a respectable soldier.

The beggar, seeing the soldier espying him, attempted his services.

"Dear soldier, I see you are hard at your duty. Would you be so kind as to let this poor old man enter your great kingdom's gates and be the recipient of your people's famed mercy?"

The soldier bellowed down at the beggar from his post, which was a mere built-in windowed ledge situated halfway down the fifty-foot high stone wall. He yelled far louder than was needed in order to be heard, even by an elderly man:

"By order of the King, the gates are closed and secure. No one shall enter or leave. Come back another day to find mercy."

The soldier was too high above to see the beggar's eyes flash with fire. But the beggar quickly gained his composure in reply: "But sir, have pity on a man without a place to lay his head, on a bare night that will bring cold to his meatless limbs."

The soldier was trained well. He stood his ground inside his tiny den with silence, ignoring this contemptible creature. His people might have mercy; he did not. He would not stoop so low as to repeat himself when he had spoken clearly and had clearly been understood. He stared straight ahead, not even glimpsing down in the direction of where the beggar was.

After a couple of minutes of silence, the suspense at not hearing from the beggar again was greater than his resolve and he gave a quick glance down and to his left where the beggar had last stood.

The beggar was gone and nowhere to be found! He had not seen him come and he did not see how he left. Nowhere as far as his eye could scope could he see the man! His eyes could not have fooled him. He had spoken with the man. Should he alert his post? What would he say, that a man had suddenly appeared and disappeared without his noticing? Either he would be deemed irresponsible or crazy. He decided to remain quiet. What danger could an old beggar man pose? He remained at his post. Alert. Disconcerted. Feeling as uneasy as the stormy winds in the air.

If the soldier had been on the other side of the wall, inside the kingdom, he would have spotted his beggar man, stumbling through the streets—alone and unnoticed.

The oracle sat, and then stood and paced—returned to sitting and then got up again. She was too stirred up inside to receive any guidance. Not until her own internal sea of calm was achieved would any messages or omens come. She was trying to smooth these internal waters, but the winds of change were blowing too swiftly to keep the waves unchurned.

Perhaps, she thought, *I am unable to settle them because I don't really want to see.*

With that idea she sat in the downy chair one last time before sleep finally overtook her, after a night before without any.

The King, still in his secured location within the castle, was awaiting the return of the General's report. He fidgeted with his royal suit as he played out various military strategies in his mind. Pacing the floors, he could feel death on his doorstep. As the foreboding crept up from his stomach into his chest where it threatened to choke the breath in his very throat, a knock sent the fear scurrying like a rat down to his boots where it froze him in place even as his voice, now freed, asserted, "Enter!"

The doorman bowed low as the door opened and General Morlay's security officer entered with haste, bowing quickly and decisively. The doorman reclosed the doors after the King had motioned with a nod of his head to do so, and only then did the King find his feet again. Walking forward, he spoke discreetly, "What news?"

"My liege, the General sends this," and she pulled out the military attaché from her inner pocket in the uniform, unfolded the parchment within, and after opening it, read:

> The General sends word that the only unusual item to report is an unusually high number of travelers and traders for this time of year, all in similar traveler's cloaks. I am assuming based on the report of a possible threat that this is an army in disguise, getting ready to attack without warning. My troops are gathering and arming now. We will be ready before nightfall. The gates are already secured. No one is going in or out without direct orders from you or me. I would have brought word myself but considering the possibility of imminent threat, my command is needed on the field. I await your reply.
>
> Your faithful servant,
>
> *General Morlay*

The courier folded the report and offered it to the King, whose face was as taut as the parchment, but unreadable in the dimming light. King Beon accepted the folded parchment and turned. Without a word he was across the parquet floor and through the door to his private quarters, leaving the courier standing awkwardly alone in the outer room in deafening silence.

The King strode even faster through passages designed only for him. He had one agenda only. To confer with his oracle one last time before nightfall.

The old beggar continued to stumble through the streets, unnoticed by people hurrying to take cover, close down their markets, and await out the night in their homes as the repeated official warnings had alerted them to do. As he turned a corner, he tripped on an up-angled cobblestone and went sprawling to the ground in a flurry of curses. A young boy, too young to be conscripted for the armory, let alone the army, and too sheltered to be afraid of anyone, ran across the street from his mother's last packing of the night, to help the old man. Was it his grandpapá who hadn't visited in many months? Maybe his grandpapá had come to surprise them!

The bronze-skinned, tawny-haired boy bent down to help the old man up, but the man's fall had caused his traveling cloak to totally cover him up. The boy was unsure where to put his hand to assist.

Suddenly, the old man got up, straightened himself and was about to begin walking again, when he spotted the lad in his periphery, and turned to look at him. The boy's mouth was wide open, unable to speak a word. For the old man wasn't old after all. The boy must've just wished he had seen his grandpapá.

"Go away, boy," he growled, "I don't need your help." And off he strode quickly and purposefully across the city square in the direction of the castle—still muttering curses. The boy had seen his transformation. He was only a child, though. No one would believe him when he said he'd seen an old man fall down and a young man get up.

As the man made his way closer to the castle, his steps were sure, his eyes focused on the path to a door he knew all too well. Upon approaching the door, hidden behind a large oaken tree he pulled out a key hung around his neck with a chain and put it into the lock. It turned and clicked as smoothly as a well-made timepiece. Looking around at the mostly deserted streets to make sure not even a young lad was watching him this time, he quickly and without a sound opened the door and slid in unseen. Locking the door behind him, he found himself in an outer walkway. There was only one person in the entire realm he did not wish to see. Only one person could bring down his entire plan, but he needed to stay in his natural form to conserve his energy for any needed escape.

He walked briskly and yet with an air of focused calm. He did not want anyone to think he was hurrying or lingering—either attracted suspicion.

However, the stone portico was more deserted than the streets. As he passed familiar buildings with more doors and more walkways, the maze of the castle could have been his doom, but he walked on, assured of his path.

Passing a guard after his next turn he nodded and spoke genially, "Good evening."

The guard nodded. He had seen this man before. There was no cause for alarm.

The caped man turned left at the next building, took two more rights and in a moment came to a second locked door. He again pulled off a neck chain and opened the door easily with a second key. He was now within the castle itself—a large meandering stone mansion with many turrets and even more doors and passageways. His target was close at hand. He found himself there with twenty short steps and a left turn—a locked door at the bottom of a long spiraling stairway that led to the top of a tower.

He pulled out a second chain of keys, opened the first door and quietly he stole up to the next door. He had marked carefully which key went to each door so there could be no mistake. He could not afford even one.

As he came to the second door, he rapped a rhythmic knock. The window was opened from the inside and the sentry looked through it at the handsome man standing on the other side of the door.

"Who are you?"

"I'm a friend of Havorth. Are you going to ask me the riddle so I can go through?"

"Where's Havorth? Only Havorth uses this door."

"He has been sent out on urgent business by the King for a military communiqué because of the impending attack. Surely you have heard the kingdom is under threat?"

"Of course I have. I'm a sentry. I receive all news of general threat." The sentry was annoyed. He was of importance though Havorth often treated him as a fool. He had no idea, though, he was being easily manipulated.

"Yes, yes, of course you would," the man replied glibly, calming the man's ruffled feathers, "Havorth has given me the keys and the passwords to escort the lady-in-white to a safe location. He would not have given me these things except that he totally trusts me. You know Havorth—he would never give these away without total trust."

"True, but this is highly unusual. No one but Havorth has ever come through these doors, except for the King himself!"

"These are highly unusual times. It is urgent that the lady-in-white be protected."

The sentry thought for a few moments and then asked the man the first riddle.

The stranger answered effortlessly.

The sentry rubbed his forehead where sweat drops had started to appear like dew on a moist morning. This man knew the riddle. Clearly, this man also had the right keys and knew how to use them correctly. As the sentry pondered whether he should continue to the next question, a thought occurred to him that gave him strength and he fired away the next riddle.

The chiseled face again had no trouble answering it, so the sentry opened the door from his side and bid him farewell as the stranger began to climb the stairs behind him.

As the unusual character reached the next doors he found and used the keys easily. The next sentry at the fifth door proved himself easier than the keys. This sentry figured it was none of his business who came through the doors. For all he knew, Havorth was dead. If a stranger knew the knocks, the answers to the riddles and had the keys, it wasn't his job to suspect him of anything—only to unlock the door for the one with the word keys and the actual keys.

And so he did and after he heard the upper floor door unlock and close again, he went back to his solitary card game—the pastime of sentries locked up in towers with nothing to do.

The stranger ascended one more floor and then he was at the last door, the door that would finally bring his purpose. As he made his entrance he was prepared for an attack. She was a seer after all. She may have seen his entrance and hidden. He could sense nothing, hear nothing, see nothing. He had his own skills, though. He closed his eyes and extended his thought, his mind, his energy into the first room, focusing it like a ray of light. Wherever she was, his energy would sense it. The first room was empty. He was sure of it. He continued to scan, creating a web of energy into the surrounding rooms and closets, extending it wherever he sensed an opening. But he could not pick up her energy. Perhaps she knew how to shield her presence? Maybe she could evade his web through a powerful transformation of her own?

He had been warned she was beyond him, but he had scoffed at this. How could she be beyond him? He had studied with a great sorcerer, unknown to his world except through invitation and a series of excruciating trials and tests. He was his best student in fifty years. No one else could do what he could. How could this unlearned orphan girl be beyond him?

Now he was angry. He withdrew his web after no success and began running throughout the residence overturning tables, throwing open doors, upending anything that got in his way. Finding a door to an outer windowed terrace, he raced up to the pool of waters—troubled and stirring. She was nowhere. His efforts were pointless. His sorcery worthless to him now. She was not here where his sources had confirmed her to be.

He flew down the stairs in a fury. He had left the doors unlocked for a quick escape. The uppermost sentry at the fifth floor barely looked at him as he passed through, but the second sentry at the second floor was gone. He had no key to this door! He was trapped. He was sure the fifth-floor sentry would not reallow him entry. It was too odd even for his passive nature. He would suspect something, and he could not risk being found out by yet another person. Panic, an unusual sensation he had rarely felt began to penetrate like cold venom through his body. He had not foreseen his doom—only the King's and the oracle's. How could he have misread the signs and the omens?

His mind offered up one unworkable solution after another. And then he had his plan.

Chapter Seven

While the intruder had made his way through the next doorways, the sentry had quickly begun constructing a chain of cards. With a few tears in each card and a flag punched through the last card, he went through his second door, locking it from the reverse side. Between the second and third doors then, he had trapped the intruder. There was no way for the interloper to escape. He then lowered his card chain out the tiny window that he knew was right above Havorth's residential window. He lowered the card chain as quickly as he dared, without risking a card getting dislodged and falling. The sentry let the card chain hang where he thought Havorth's window was, pulling the card chain up and down in case he didn't have the distance quite right. Havorth might see it in motion. He kept at it, waiting with his breath caught in his throat, silent and unmoving, listening for the stranger's return. Very soon after lowering the chain, within seconds—though it felt like an æon—the card chain yanked. Havorth had seen it!

It took less than two minutes. Havorth knew because his timepiece, accurate to within a second over the span of a year, showed this to be true. He arrived at the first door of the tower after seeing and yanking on the card chain out his window. He hadn't known what it meant, but twice in one day, he'd been messaged in unusual ways. Something was stirring. His annoyance and curiosity were enough at odds with each other to compel him to investigate. Havorth startled when he saw the sentry right in front of the first door.

"Why did you call me here? Why are you at the first door and not at your post?" Havorth asked accusatorily.

He shouldn't be surprised, thought the sentry. *The only window I could have lowered my card chain out of was in this part of the stairwell. As high and mighty as Havorth thinks he is, he's sometimes very dumb.* "There is a stranger who is up the stairs," he explained. "I presume all the way up the tower since I heard more doors opening and closing above me. He had the keys and the answers to the riddles. He said you gave them to him to escort the lady-in-white to safety. I locked him behind the second door so he can't make his escape back down."

Havorth's eyes widened and he took a step back.

"How can this be? I have my keys with me. Here!" and Havorth pulled the keys out of his pocket to show the sentry, to prove his words, unexpectedly afraid the sentry wouldn't believe him.

"What about the lady-in-white? Should we go and save her?" the sentry fidgeted as he contemplated confronting the stranger.

"No. We're probably too late for that," Havorth responded, looking down. "If he wanted access to the lady-in-white, he's got that already. If he's harmed her, he's harmed her. He'll be needing escape. If he hasn't harmed her, he'll be wanting to escape with her. Either way, the most important thing we can do now is to prevent his escape.

"Let's stay behind this door and decide what to do from here. Whoever the stranger is, he's trapped for now," Havorth strategized, rubbing his stubby hands over and over his balding head as if he thought this would spark some genius—like polishing a stone would bring out its brilliance.

The sentry felt his chest expand, proudly. Havorth did not know who the stranger was. He had concluded correctly: The stranger was a trespasser. And a liar.

The first thing Havorth decided to do was to check the King's keys to make sure they had not been stolen. Leaving the sentry there, Havorth raced as fast as his short legs would take him down to the King's quarters. He convinced the guard to double check the King's keys. Finding they were there, Havorth raced back—not as quickly.

The sentry added, "I think we need more help. What if he has weapons? What if he has the lady-in-white as a hostage?"

Havorth nodded, agreeing with the sentry. "Let's see if we can gather some more guards," Havorth added. This time, they both took off in different directions to try to round up as many guards as possible.

When they'd met back, they found that under the current high alert, none of the guards could leave their posts without a direct order from a superior. And they knew there was no time to find a superior and enact a chain of command.

Havorth puzzled: "Clearly the guards are of no use to us. What do we have that we can use to apprehend the intruder ourselves?"

For all his smarts, Havorth is really useless when it comes to a crisis, the sentry thought to himself. However, he kept his thoughts to himself again and said, "The sentry closet has shackles and other materials that might be possible to restrain the intruder."

"Great idea! Let's go at once!" and Havorth strode off. The sentry caught up to him quickly—his longer legs made that an easy endeavor.

Once at the closet, the sentry unlocked the door as he was the only one with the key this time. There was not much to be found: a mop, a pail, a broom, lots of playing cards, and trays and vessels for food and drink. The shackles were missing. But there was also rope—lots of it. Havorth and the sentry both grabbed at it. There was enough for both. Havorth quickly strode back to the tower without a word leaving the sentry to lock the door and catch up again.

Once he had, Havorth began, "I think the best use of each of us is for me to unlock the second door once we are there, and for you to be ready to spring through the door with the only element of surprise we have. He may only be expecting you, not two of us. You make way to tackle him since you are bigger than I, then I will follow in behind you and tie up his legs. Then together we'll force his hands to tie them at once. Just do not allow him the upper hand. Guard your neck in the fight."

44

The sentry rolled his eyes to himself. What was a sentry that was not trained in hand-to-hand combat? Havorth knew nothing of these matters, he was sure. He would gain the upper hand easily. That was one of the reasons he had been chosen as a select sentry for the secret turret. He could outwrestle the best of most who were in the King's army.

They were soon back at the first door. Havorth opened it easily and the sentry handed him the key to the second door as they climbed the stairs as quietly as possible. The intruder may have heard the unlocking of the first door, but they had no other choice then to strive for stealthy movement regardless. If the intruder were there, he would definitely hear them unlock the second door, so the sentry had to act quickly. Decisively. Like a wild forest cat he had once observed attacking a deer.

With the clunk of the unlocking mechanism, the sentry stood at the edge of the door, ready to pounce. The hinge creaked, and hurriedly, Havorth opened the door. The sentry ran at the intruder, who was indeed there, but oddly, was hunched in a corner beneath his cloak.

The sentry leapt into the air in order to tackle the huddled mass. But just as he was about to land on the intruder's back, the intruder spun in a blurring mass. The sentry reached out his hand to secure his hold on the man. It was no use. The spinning bundle of cloak and man had moved to the side just enough so that the sentry landed hard on the concrete floor and steps, hitting his head on a stone step. Sprawled and stunned by the impact, he lay there momentarily knocked unconscious.

Havorth, seeing the intruder was moving toward him and the door, dropped the rope and ran at the still spinning mass. But just as he was about to grab it, the mass moved to the side again, and rose into the air in a whirl of gray and black. Havorth, still running in the trajectory of his aim, reached out to the side to try and clutch the intruder's cloak. Alas, his arms were too short and the cloak was already gone. All that remained was a black raven of enormous size, dappled with gray over its back and a beak that looked more like a man's nose. It squawked a terrible screech, and then dove toward the open door.

The sentry opened his eyes in time to see a giant raven fly out the door.

In their hurry, they had left the first door open and out of his peripheral vision, Havorth spied the raven fly through that door and into the windowless hall. *We might still catch him!* he thought.

Helping the still-stunned sentry up, Havorth ran after the raptor. As the sentry slunk along behind as quickly as he could without going dizzy again, Havorth yelled, "Help!"

The guard near the door at the end of the hall heard the cry for help and looked down the hall to his right to see a dark form flying toward him. *How did a bird that size get into the castle?*

Not sure what they needed help with, except to aid in the bird finding its way out, the guard opened the door. The raven flew through it and out and away with Havorth yelling as he ran fruitlessly towards the door, "No-o-o!!!"

A split second later, the sentry—who even disabled could nearly keep up with the diminutive escort—arrived at the open door just in time to see the raven flying higher and away over Devor's homes. He and Havorth gaped as the bird winged over their kingdom-city walls and out of sight. Havorth turned and stared at the sentry who also turned and stared back in shock.

Havorth didn't know whether the sentry had seen the intruder's transformation or not, but he could see the sentry looked as dumbstruck as he thought he himself must look and feel. *No*, thought Havorth, *No, I feel worse.*

For just before the intruder had transfigured itself…

But how? How was such a thing possible?

He must've imagined it. But he couldn't have. Both he and the sentry had chased the bird. And it made sense. Only he and the King had keys so if someone had copies, it might have been copies from his own keys. And if they had been from his, the only person who...

No! No! It could not be.

But there was no denying it. He'd seen a glimpse of the intruder's face just before the intruder had turned into a raven.

Chapter Eight

General Morlay had assembled his troops in strategic zones around the kingdom-city's walls. They were ready. The half moon hung in the graying sky. The air was still. Too still. No one stirred. It was as if time itself was waiting. No one dared breathe. There was no sign of attack. No sign of an army. No sign of anything. The travelers that had been spotted earlier had either hidden behind hills and in the trees of the forests that surrounded the fields around the kingdom or had simply been travelers after all and had moved through the area.

Dusk was not far off. The General hoped the attack, if one was coming, was before all sight diminished with the light. *At least my troops are ready*, he repeated to himself again.

After a few more minutes of impenetrable silence, a yell went up. Then many yells. They were coming from the other side of the kingdom-city. Morlay cursed. Astride his inky stallion in two paces and a hop, he was galloping toward the commotion as fast as his trusted steed could carry him.

Then he saw it. A flare? No. It was larger than that. Much larger. A huge ball of fire flew through the sky. And then another one came, rising and arcing over the high but now useless walls.

Our enemies are attacking without even showing their faces! The cowardice! He drove his stallion, black as lava, ever harder. *What is this new devilry? Flying fire? Flaming arrows—not unusual. But giant fireballs?* He had never seen or heard of fire that was as big as a house and could fly as easily as a bird. How could they stop it?

Now he was close enough to hear the screams of villagers inside the kingdom walls. He could not concern himself with them at the moment. He had to drive to his soldiers who would await his command.

The increasingly darkening sky was now lit up with fire balls. He could hold off no longer. The squadron leaders would need to think for themselves. He blew his horn with one long blast. He followed it with another long blast, even louder this time. They would charge. The command would carry around the walls by soldiers at the top of the wall who would blast their horns in the same cadence he had used.

Moments later he arrived at the battle station where the first fireballs had been sighted. The soldiers, girded and armed with arrows, battle axes, and spears, were already charging in the direction the fireballs had originated as the horn blasts had commanded. General Morlay rode after the running battalion, quickly taking the lead. They still could see no one. No army. No general. They ran and rode blind.

It was clear to Morlay that his soldiers would be running into the woods where whoever was attacking would be well hidden and prepared for battle. They had no choice, though. The firebombs would continue until they stopped the attackers directly. They continued to charge into all the surrounding forest and still they saw no one.

Morlay was feeling desperate. Where was this ghost army? If they went too deeply into the forest they could easily be surrounded and attacked from the rear. He rode ahead of this squadron of soldiers in the flank of that southeast trajectory from the kingdom. He could tell his troops were confused, anxious, yet determined. Then he saw a sudden movement. How could he have? They were in the dark of the woods. A few torches could barely shine the light a few feet ahead of the front line. Then he saw it again. Up ahead, someone, something was moving, running. Another fireball went up and everything was illumined for a few brief seconds.

Several hundred feet away was a large clearing. Men were running into the woods on the far side of the clearing, away from some sort of catapulting machine that was in the middle of the clearing. It was most definitely the source of the sling-shotted fireballs. But it was in flames and the trees at the far side of the clearing were now on fire as well, preventing the General and his troops from pursuing their attackers. In a matter of minutes, the entire forest could be aflame.

He signaled a stop. His faithful horse, Latticer, obeyed his order, too, sniffing the smoke, sensing the fire. As he held fast, momentarily taking it all in at once, he saw the beginning inferno was spreading rapidly. He had to get his army out of there. "Retreat! Retreat!" he yelled, blowing two short blasts on his horn as loudly as he could. Immediately obeying orders, the soldiers ran back through the same woods they had just charged through.

The fire made his skin tingle, his perceptions more vivid. He looked around as he followed up the rear of his flank. The trees were lit like candles—a flame on top, spreading from one to another—creating a vast canopy of fire. It had been a dry year. The entire forest would go. The brilliance of the kingdom-city's safety—built in the middle of a vast clearing in the midst of an even vaster surrounding forest— could also be its undoing.

The kingdom-city was safe from the burning forest for now. The fires could not reach past the grounds and the walls. But the kingdom-city's natural territorial wall would soon be gone. Then it hit him, hard—like a hammer to the head: The city inside was on fire, too!

As his soldiers reached the circumscribed clearing around the kingdom's walls, General Morlay could see that his commanders of other flanks had experienced the same reality as well and they were in retreat, running out of the woods, like them.

Now that they were all running back to Devor, with the enemy running away in the opposite direction, the next demand would be putting out the fires inside the walls using the water from the river and the trenches. This was their immediate priority. The fleeing attackers could be dealt with another day. They were no longer a threat. After sending a volley of fireballs, they had burnt their machines and the trees to prevent capture of men or technology.

He charged ahead, blowing his horn three times and then yelling a command. "Divide up. Half of you, gather water and flood the grounds outside and half go inside and help put out the fires inside. I will stay outside to make sure another attack does not come." His troops followed his orders without hesitation. It was a night that for General Morlay and his soldiers, did not end.

The kingdom was ablaze. Flames shot high into the charred sky. Fear struck deep in the King's chest as if the ever-tightening snake of dread coiled around his neck had slithered down and bitten his heart like a venomous asp. He pushed the pain aside, riding his own steed full speed. His horse was terrified of the fire, the King could sense it like his own fear. But well-trained and loyal, his horse would not leave the King nor step aside of the King's command.

King Beon raced to different areas of the kingdom ordering his troops like he hoped his General was doing outside the kingdom walls. They had had no communication since the fire balls had begun. He had heard the horns. He could only imagine the battle happening outside the walls.

"Bring water to the northeast part of the kingdom—now!" bellowed the King.

"Yes, your majesty," soldiers responded to each and every command that was always the same.

He pushed his fear and the nightmarish images to the side of his mind and continued riding and giving orders for water to be delivered to new fires. Chaos ensued. People were running and screaming. Then, in an instant, the fireballs that had flown from the sky and fallen throughout the kingdom stopped. No more fire fell. The raging fires within the kingdom-city were still rapidly spreading and most were not even close to being under control, but many could be if the fireballs had stopped.

Good. My General has been successful. Thanks be to the Devorah. As he rode back to the castle to check on its well-being, he remembered Edora—she had foreseen all of this. She was safe; he was sure of it, but how much worse could this attack have been had her gifts not foretold these events?

Then the asp struck the king's heart again. Edora had said his family—the royal line— was at risk. His wife was gone, and they'd had no children. The next in line to the throne were cousins—daughters of his elderly cousins—all wise and well-educated. His only relatives. Where were they? In the chaos and fury of the fire attack, he had not checked on their safety.

He turned his steed around racing to their house near the northwest corner on the other side of the castle. He hoped they had taken refuge in the stone castle. Their house, like most of the houses in the kingdom-city, was thatched and wooden—exceedingly vulnerable to fire. He raced faster, not needing to drive his horse who seemed relieved to be running away from the center of the fire storms—and was galloping as if his own life depended on it.

The King and his royally-bred ride rounded the far corner of the castle. There he saw the worst possible sight he had ever seen. His cousins' house was no longer. Charred and already burnt to the ground it must have been one of the first hit by a fireball. There would have been no warning. By alerting the kingdom to the possible attack, everyone had gone, as they should have, to the inside of their homes, making them at greater risk to the fireballs than if they had been wandering the streets. As he neared, desperate for any sign of life, he heard wailing coming from behind a nearby house. He made his way closer to the sound and found an old woman kneeling in the dirt, tearing at her gray hair and singed clothes.

"Woman, who are you? Are you injured? How may I assist you?" the King queried urgently.

"My liege, my liege, they're all dead. All of them."

"Who? Who is dead?"

"Your kin. I am their cook." She gasped for breath and began rocking back and forth on her haunches, wailing even louder.

King Beon froze. He tried to speak, to console this grief-stricken old woman but his tongue was as thick and heavy as a woolen blanket. His mind, too, felt like stagnant water had just flooded it, preventing any ability to make a linear thought. "All dead" were the only words that managed to pop out of his swollen mouth from his deluged brain.

After a few moments of stunned silence, the King's horse whinnied at the delay, clearing the King's temporary shock. He dismounted and went to the maid's side, speaking softly, he whispered, "You are sure?"

"Yes, my liege. They were all inside, the parents and their daughters. I went out for a quick check on the neighbors as your cousins requested of me, since the neighbors have young children and the father is out with the troops." Her speaking faltered; she began to whimper. As she broke into words again, her voice wailed through the words, her grief thinly veiled. "Then while I was there, I heard a massive explosion and ran back out of the neighbor's house to see your cousins' house totally in flames. No one got out. No one. They're all dead. All dead." Her words were mere whispers now, as if speaking loudly might disturb the spirits who had left their bodies.

"Dear woman, what is your name. Do you have family you can go to?"

"Yes, yes, my liege. I am Elegh. My sister lives on the other side of the city. Is it safe to go?"

"I believe so. The firebombs have stopped for now. Make haste to check on your sister."

"Thank you, my liege. I am so sorry for your kin, for your loss."

"We all have lost this evening. If you need work after tonight, please return to the castle and submit your name as a cook. I will take you in after your diligent service to my cousins."

"Thank you. Thank you. May the Devorah bless you," and with a curtsy and a bow she retreated and started walking in the direction of her sister's home, still moaning and wailing in more muted tones now.

The King nodded, strode back purposefully to his steed, and with one swift sweeping motion he was atop and galloping back to the castle's main entrance to help command the troops putting out the lingering fires.

Chapter Nine

BEFORE THE FIREBOMBS

The King entered Edora's tower by a passage unknown even to her, one he'd kept secret for just such a time as this. An interior ladder led up to a secret door in a cabinet only he had keys for, which when unlocked from the inside, opened into the center room of the tower.

Upon seeing Edora asleep, King Beon had gently but firmly shaken her shoulder. She yelped in fright upon seeing him standing next to her so unexpectedly, and because he'd awakened her from a fitful nap filled with dreams of fires and screams.

"I'm sorry to frighten you, Edora. We need to leave. Now," he whispered.

His face was taut with lines of worry. Noticing the light dimming, nearing dusk, she wondered to herself, *How long have I slept? Is there a battle being waged? Or is it all over?*

The answers would have to wait for the time being as the King gestured silence with a single finger to his lips and led Edora back to the secret cabinet after she had quickly grabbed a few essentials. *How had I never known about this? I am an oracle, after all. Couldn't I have seen this? What else is the King keeping secret?*

She stepped onto the ladder first and began climbing down with the King doing the same above her after he had closed and locked the cabinet from the inside. At the bottom of the long, wooden ladder, Edora found herself in a subterranean corridor. Dimly lit with torches, the dirty cobblestone path looked like it was rarely used. When the King had stepped off the ladder, he again gestured silence, as if he knew Edora was ready to launch into a million questions and led her away into the even darker hall.

A few minutes later after many twisting turns with forked paths, they reached a heavily ornate wooden door, carved with the markings she knew so well: the personal emblems of the King. King Beon brought out another key, unlocked the door, and without a squeak, the door swung on its large metal hinges to reveal a vast, well-appointed room. If it had been above ground Edora would have thought it was part of the King's quarters, as regal furniture anchored the space. Below ground, it felt inhospitable and uncomfortable—more like death—as in a well-appointed royal crypt.

Once the King had bolted the door behind him, he finally spoke, but in hushed tones. "Edora. You will be safe here. You will find everything you need. Food is within this cupboard and through the passageway over here, you will find a well for water and a bed should sleep overtake you. I've set some tea out that I made before I retrieved you," he said pointing to a large earthen mug set on a small, metal table next to a brocade chaise lounge.

"No one besides my private footman knows of this room and even he is unaware of the passageway that connects this room to your tower. This is my safe house. My footman will not come here unless by my order or unless I am missing and cannot be summoned or found. I will tell him on my way out that if something happens to me in this battle that there is a great treasure here he must retrieve immediately and bring to safety. He is of the utmost caliber. I trust him with my life. And with yours…"

"My King, so the battle has not even started yet? I've seen it in my dreams as I just slept and did not understand if they were the future or the present."

"No, there has been no battle nor any indication of an army approaching, just bands of travelers that are high in number for this time of year. But you believe, then, the battle still approaches?"

"Yes, it was ever present in my dreams, my King. But why must I stay here? The tower is safe, surely? It has always been safe in years past."

"Please, Edora, after all these years, you may call me 'Beon.' I consult you after all. I am hardly your King. But let me assure you, that you are safer here than anywhere, even than your tower which has windows. Someone who is unfriendly in the coming battle may spot you and find a way to bring you harm. I know not what this eve and the morrow may bring, but my Niamà, on her deathbed, foretold me to keep you safe. So, I am fulfilling my deathbed promise to her to keep you as safe as I could keep myself."

"My King, I mean, excuse me, King Beon," she couldn't bring herself to merely call him Beon. It was far too familiar. Theirs was a formal relationship, even if he came to her, she was providing a service to the King. "You have never told me of Niamà. Who was she?"

"I will have to tell you another time, Edora. For now, I must return to the castle grounds to keep charge within the walls, while my General awaits outside of them."

The King walked over to the fireplace and with a flint and some dry hay set to the side, he started a fire with the sticks and logs that were already laid up for a fire.

"This should chase away the damp and chill and give you some light to keep the night not so dark. I am off. Be well, Edora."

"Thank you, my King, Beon," Edora said with her heart open and full.

With that the King left through the same door they had come through. With a clunk of the lock, Edora was again alone.

She had not dared to say it to the King, but she had wanted to yell out, "Not a fire! No fire in the fireplace!" She had never told him that in her troubled visions and dreams, it was fire that undid his line. She was too afraid to speak the horrors she had seen, and so she had quelled her voice before it had burst out uncontrolled.

She walked to the chaise lounge against the wall opposite the fireplace. Moving it so it faced toward the door leading to the secret passageway and away from the fire, she lay down on it and picked up the earthenware mug of steaming, steeped russlet tree leaves, sipping on it gently. Willing herself not to see the abundant fire now flaming in its box in her periphery, she looked straight ahead. Fire was all she had seen whenever she closed her eyes, and she didn't want the infernal images to continue dancing in front of her open eyes—real and right in front of her.

The stone walls were covered with tapestries in a hopeless attempt to warm up the space, Edora thought. It only made her feel closed in and suffocated. Would she die here? Would the King die? Her heart, though tense and afraid at what would befall them all in the night was strangely warmed. Maybe the hot tea the King had set out for her was medicinal. A tingling spread throughout her body and with the heat the blazing fire provided, she was soon asleep, eventually dreaming again of fire and screams—her own this time.

Edora awoke, shaking from the tortured scenes replaying themselves over and over again in her head. The flames in the fireplace were still awake and dancing. She hated fire. It was a necessary evil, but an evil. Her life had been marked by fire. Fire and fleeing. Villagers had threatened to burn her mamá at the stake for her prophecy. Fleeing from that threat of fire had cost them their dear papá. She and her mamá had awoken in the night to a burning barn. They barely escaped. Her mamá's lungs, singed by the smoke, never healed, and living and begging along the roadside led to her mamá's untimely death within a few weeks. As she held her dear mamá on an early winter morning under a tree-shaded shanty not too far from Devor, her mamá's lungs gasping and wheezing, she spoke her final words, "Edora, I am soon to leave this world. Your future is bright. So bright. I can see it all. You will make your mark on this world, sweet Edora. I will miss you so. Do not mourn for long. Keep moving. I and your papá will always be with you. We will make our spirits known to you from the overworld when needed." Her words were labored and slow. "There is one time far in the future that will be very dark. So dark. You will survive it. You will."

"Mamá, be gentle. Don't talk so much, mamá. Save your breath, your energy. I love you my mamá. Don't talk of leaving me. I can't bear it. Please. Stay here with me."

"Edora, my love, you are my greatest gift to the world. Do not be afraid. The overworld will guide you. Oh!" and her eyes widened to fully receive what she could only see. "Oh, your papá is here, Edora! I can see him."

"Mamá!"

"Oh, Love!" and with a last gasp her mamá was gone. She couldn't see her papá but her mamá's soul floated above her body like a feather, hovering as if to stay and console her orphan, but then a gust of wind rushed through the shanty and her soul was carried away on its breath.

Edora was left alone. The tears burned, just as fire had burned her life to ashes again and again.

As she gazed at the fire now, feeling the dreaded, destructive waves of heat emanating from the fireplace, remembering her losses, the tears fell again as her heart mourned. What other losses would be hers tonight? What losses would her beloved Devor incur—the place she had finally found some peace and solace?

She got up off the chaise and paced the rug-covered floors. Could she see if she gathered some waters? Did she want to see? Her physical eyes could see nothing in this underground prison. She could hear nothing. If she was going to find out what, if anything, was happening outside these walls, she would have to risk the scrying waters.

Making her way through the passageway the King had pointed out to her, her steps muffled by the fabric on walls and floors, she thought to herself: *No one would ever know I was in here. No one would ever know to rescue me in here if the kingdom with the most excellent footman goes up in flames.*

As she made her way into the side room, she noticed the elegant bed: dressed in fine burgundy and blue brocades, trimmed with satin and lace. The King settled for nothing less than the usual royal treatments, even in his safe house. Having moved away from the fireplace, she shivered in the cold room. A handpump well was driven straight into the ground in the corner of the room and atop the dresser beside the bed was a solid-cobalt porcelain pitcher with basin.

She took the pitcher over to the well and began priming it. After a few strokes, it filled with water and putting the pitcher under the spout, she pumped it lightly until the pitcher was full. Then she walked over to the dressing table and poured the water into the basin about halfway to the brim.

The waters, freshly poured, shimmered as if expecting some magick. Edora had left her wand behind in the tower, but she put her hands over the basin and pronounced, louder than normal to assuage her unease and her uncertainty,

> In scrying waters I do see
> a picture of reality.
> Be to me a looking glass
> for with to tell is all I ask.

The energy from her hands swirled down and began to stir the waters. Foaming and bubbling she removed her hands looking deeply into the watery abyss.

Chapter Ten

AFTER THE FIREBOMBS

For days, the air was filled with acrid smoke and ashes that fell from the skies like charcoal snow. The forest fires that had been set by the fleeing attackers had burned the trees in their entirety. However, the fires had ultimately been stopped by a wide, vast clearing between the circling forest and Devor. The General had watered the outside grounds until they were practically flooded, and it had been enough to keep the forest fire from jumping onto kingdom flora. The inside of the kingdom-city, though, had suffered from a number of fires. It was estimated that somewhere between twenty to thirty firebombs had been catapulted inside the kingdom. The castle itself was unharmed. The loss of life stood small, at about three dozen, with burns and injuries numbering a few dozen more. All in all, they had survived intact. The Shandar forest was no longer and could no longer be counted on as a natural shield. The trees beyond the Shandar were spared by a sudden, severe rainstorm that had mercifully blocked extensive damage into surrounding regions.

These were the King's assessments. Of course, his known line was gone. There were records that could trace a more distant relative that would someday take his place, but that would have to wait. His more urgent matter was finding out who the attackers were and why Edora seemed to have been a target. And how in all the matters of kingdom security his own scribe seemed to be the weak link in the chain was what vexed him most of all.

King Beon along with General Morlay made haste to convene a security council meeting that would consider these matters.

When the security council convened two days later, the King sat at the head of the long, wooden table carved with symbols of all the kings and queens who had gone before him. At his right hand sat his General who, when the assembly had gathered, rose and commenced the meeting with a speech.

"Your highness, the twentieth King of Devor, my liege," he nodded in the King's direction and then took in the entire assembly with his gaze. "To all who are gathered here, the King and I are grateful for your dedicated service in the recent fire attack on Devor. Let it be said that we withstood a grave danger and a cowardly enemy and remain in good stead despite our casualties, the losses of the forest and several homes.

"The trees of the Shandar Forest were our best natural defense. Now that the forest is gone, we are more vulnerable than ever to another attack, although another firebombing would not be likely as there is no forest to provide them cover or fuel for the fire. There is one benefit as now we would see any attack coming, but because this enemy is cowardly, I do not believe they would attempt a visible attack in any case. By estimate of the troop leaders, their numbers were very low especially compared to ours. This gave them the advantage, hiding in trees, but now that advantage is gone. However, we must make haste to fortify our defenses and extend our lookouts since our best natural barrier is no more.

"There is no known current enemy of Devor. All our treaties remain intact, so a more urgent matter is to discover who has attacked us and why. We know nothing of them. They, however, appear to know a great deal about us. The most urgent of all is how. How do they know so much of us when we know nothing of them? How did an intruder, presumably one of the attackers, gain entry to a private chamber of the castle with the keys and riddle answers to do so?

"I and two others have interrogated our liege's scribe, Havorth, the only known person other than the King himself who has the keys to the secret chamber. We have also questioned the two sentries on duty at the time of the intrusion and a lone guard who witnessed the final events. This lone guard had little to tell as he saw no one leave or try to escape but simply Havorth and one of the sentries running after a bird. The other sentry had little to contribute, as he was unaware that the intruder even was an intruder and could only provide a description of the man and a brief account of events that involved him. The scribe and the other sentry were more involved, as you will hear—their tales coincide exactly, so I will only have

Havorth himself recount his experience with you today. As precisely as the scribe and the one sentry's accounts match, I do believe they are withholding information. I do not know if they are traitors who helped the intruder or are both imbeciles who are ashamed of their inability to detain the intruder and are withholding details of their mutual ineptitude in the course of events. I will let this council decide after hearing him out and then questioning Havorth for yourselves."

The General looked steadily at everyone at the table and upon seeing in their eyes the resolve to find the needed answers he glanced at the King. The King seeing the General's gaze directed at him decided not to match it, but instead gave a heavy sigh at the unpleasant task before them. If the King's own scribe was treacherous at worst or incompetent at best, either way the interrogation would reveal that his trust was misplaced. This would have many implications for the ordering of power in the kingdom. King Beon knew it and he knew his General knew it. And so, rather than match his gaze, he averted it to the doors through which Havorth would soon enter.

The General, following the King's mind, then looked at the doorman and commanded tersely, "Let him in."

The doorman bowed, opened the large doors that led into the Great Room, and summoned entry to the small man quaking behind the doors with a guard beside him. After Havorth had made his way to the Great Table, he was motioned to sit at the center of the left side of the King. Tall rectangular leaded windows, glazed and backlit with smoky sunlight, shone through with rays of light that bounced on his balding head as he sat in the tall chair designated for him. The military council on his either side, dwarfed Havorth in size. *He looks like a frightened child*, the King thought to himself. *I hope for his sake he has nothing to hide.*

General Morlay's displeasure grew as he gazed at the scribe—the General's forehead as tense as his chiseled body was in his stiff chair amid this grim duty.

"Havorth, you have previously given a statement to two of my council and myself. Would you please restate your version of the night of the attack. We will then ask you questions to gain more clarity," Morlay narrowed his eyes at Havorth while talking.

The newly appointed temporary scribe across from Havorth picked up his pen, dipped it in ink, and looked eager to begin etching the prior scribe's words onto parchment.

A little too eager, thought Havorth, as he grimaced at his replacement and began repeating his statement, yet again, this time to the council.

The Scribe's Testimony to the Council:

"As I made my way to the tower stairs with the sentry, I was beside myself with worry. I had no idea who could've copied the keys and gained entry through knowledge of the riddles. Before the sentry and I made haste to apprehend the intruder I checked the King's keys and my own to ensure that all were accounted for. They were. If there was someone else who had a set of keys, I have no idea who that could be.

"Thank the Devorah the sentry had enough wits about him to drop a red flag down to my window with a quick card chain he had made. If I hadn't been right by that window when it appeared, and being keen of eye, spotted it right away even in the dying light, well I'm sure it could have resulted in a much worse scenario.

"After seeing the flag, I yanked on it to let him know I was on my way, and I hurried up to the first door where the sentry had positioned himself. He quickly told me about the intruder up above. I immediately brought the sentry down the stairs past the first door, locking yet another door behind the intruder so he stayed trapped. We checked the King's keys then and I had my keys with me. We conspired to gather a guard or two to help us but because of the threat of attack, the guards were ordered to stay at their posts, and we did not have the authority to remove them so we were left to our own devices. We then hastened to the sentry shack to gather whatever shackles might be stored there. We found some rope but that was all.

"As we raced back to the tower, we strategized that I would unlock the door and the sentry would jump him in surprise as soon as the door was open, the sentry being a much larger presence and stronger physique than I could provide. Then, upon the commencement of tackling, I was to run in and tie the intruder's ankles, preventing his escape and then help the sentry in securing his hands as well.

"However, as soon as we opened the door, the intruder had the upper hand. Hidden under his cloak, he spun in a blur, causing the sentry to fall and knock his head. In an instant, the intruder ran by the both of us out the door, and down and out the first door which we had left unsecured in our haste. After the brief moment of being stunned, we ran after him. He was faster than the both of us and he was out of our sight in a matter of minutes. We alerted the castle guard that an intruder had escaped, and we helped them search the castle but found no one. What happened to him after that I cannot say except that I know the firebombs commenced a short time later. The sentry and I returned to the tower doors and locked them and then returned to the castle grounds and kingdom to be of help putting out fires."

Havorth was about to say more but stopped himself as he reasoned that too little was better than too much in this case.

After the awkward silence of many seconds, the General rose and announced, "Havorth, your testimony and the testimony of the sentry who helped you match exactly. However, the testimony of the guard at the end of the outer hall is perplexing. He reported that you and the sentry seemed to be chasing a bird, a raven—and a rather large one at that—out of the castle. And that after it flew away you then told him there was an intruder loose in the castle. How is it that you were chasing a bird when you knew there was an intruder loose?"

"Yes, sir, that is odd, isn't it?" Havorth gulped and turned molten red. "I am unsure how or why the guard thought we were chasing a bird." Havorth cleared his throat, which seemed to have closed up all on its own. "We were running down the hall after the intruder. The hallway is the only way to escape the tower after all. It was just a coincidence that there was a bird there. We have no idea how the intruder got away from us and out of the castle. We were slowed up by the sentry's head injuries and my short legs."

"The guard reported that no one ran by him during that time. How do you account for that?"

"I am sorry, sir. I cannot account for it. I have no idea how the intruder escaped. I have no idea how the intruder gained entry either."

General Morlay frowned and sat back down. Another military council member piped up. "You are the only one with keys to the tower, besides the King, but even the King doesn't have answers to the riddles as you change them without his knowledge. Is that not so?"

"Yes, sir." Havorth gulped.

"So if the intruder gained entrance it would have to be through you, yes?"

"Yes, but I would never help someone gain entrance to the tower. I would never betray my kingdom or my King!" Havorth glanced quickly to his right toward the King. King Beon noticed his glance but did not give any indication of having noticed Havorth's visual plea for help.

"Perhaps," said another council member, "someone gained access to these keys and riddles without your knowledge. Is there anyone with whom you associate that might have tricked you into revealing your secrets?"

Havorth turned and looked at the military man, shock written on his face. What was he to say now? He squirmed in his chair and then squeaked, "I know of no associates of mine who would betray me. I, of course, have many associations at home and abroad, being the King's scribe earns me contact with a good number of scribes from other kingdoms. If someone gained access to my secrets it was without my knowledge or cooperation. And that is the truth!" Havorth was practically yelling now, desperate for an end to what he considered undue torture.

The Great Room was again silent as the military council all directed the sternest of gazes at Havorth. When it was clear no one had any more questions, the General again rose. "Havorth, at this time, we have no evidence that what you are saying is true or false. However, in light of the fact that you were the only access to the keys and riddles, you can no longer be trusted as scribe or escort until it is ascertained how the intruder gained access to the tower. Seeing that this intruder may try to gain access again through you, you are not allowed to leave the kingdom without express permission of the King or myself. And you and your residence in the castle will be guarded around the clock. Is that understood?"

"Yes, sir," Havorth answered curtly. He wanted to protest his house arrest as they had no proof of his guilt, but his mind was cunning enough to know that he was escaping what could be a far worse punishment. "Thank you, sir." Havorth stood up and bowed low to the King, worry etched in his brow as if by an arrowhead. The King nodded in reply and the General called out to the doorman: "Have the guard outside the doors escort Havorth back to his residence and guard Havorth there until the guard is relieved by another."

The doorman nodded and opened the doors to allow Havorth to exit and to give the guard outside the General's instructions. Havorth retreated, face forward, until he had reached the door and turned to make his exit. When the doors had been closed again, the General turned to the King: "What say you, my liege?"

Breathing in a deep sigh of release that the interrogation was now over, he shifted in his chair and spoke firmly. "I agree with you,

General, that Havorth is hiding something. There is a gap in the testimony and his demeanor suggests he is protecting something or someone. Knowing Havorth I would guess that he is protecting himself most of all." He sat and thought for a few moment's pause. "But also knowing Havorth, he is a strict by-the-law type of man and I cannot see him betraying his most honored code for anything: money, reward, revenge, or any of the usual seducements. You are right to demote him and guard him. However, I believe there may be more going on beyond us all. I have my own," here he paused again as he searched for the right word and then said with emphasis, "*investigating* to do to find out more. Until then, let us adjourn until the morrow at the same time when we will attend to this and other security matters."

The General nodded in satisfaction that the King was not protecting his scribe and had agreed with the pronouncement of demotion and house arrest, although he wondered what investigating the King had in mind that did not include him. Nevertheless, he presented a seamless bridge from the King's statement to his own, as if nothing the King said had surprised him: "You are adjourned until the morrow at ten morning." The military council men and women all rose, and with the sound of wooden chairs scraping the stone tile floors as they moved them away from the table still in the air, they bowed to the King and saluted the General with their right hand over the heart before they turned and left.

Back in his residence Havorth paced the floors. He knew he was not in good favor at the council. How could he be? An outsider had gained entry to one of the most secret hiding places in the kingdom and the fault was entirely his. Of course, the council did not know that—yet. They suspected it, though. He knew they could smell his deceit in the air. He was sure of it. As a military council they were experienced at reading lies. He knew the sentry had told the same cover-up he had. They had both agreed neither would reveal what had really happened when they had come upon the intruder.

The sentry, upon agreeing to the cover-up, did not know that Havorth had more to hide than he. He did not know that Havorth had known who the intruder was. The sentry only knew that if he had ever revealed what had really happened, he would lose his credibility and his job. He would never be trusted again and so he had willingly gone along with Havorth's plan to claim ignorance as to how the intruder escaped.

Havorth, of course, had known the sentry would not want to reveal the truth. The truth would damn the sentry's reputation and so Havorth had exploited this sentry's weakness in order to help cover his own greater guilt. For now, it had worked. For how long, he did not know. What he should do about it, he had even less clarity.

Havorth did not know that the intruder's face had been seen by another. And this person had a plan.

Chapter Eleven

The King made haste to the safe house beneath his residence. He had the midday meal to deliver to Edora and he wanted to seek her council about what had been revealed at Havorth's questioning. On the way, he wondered whether Edora would already know what he had to tell her. He had rarely surprised her. The inner ladder to her tower was the only thing he believed had ever escaped her vast visionary abilities.

He had brought her each and every meal since hiding her there two days ago. No one knew where she was and he wanted it kept that way for now, until he and they knew more about the mysterious intruder and his band of fire attackers.

At the bottom of the secret staircase that descended directly from his bedroom closet into his hidden underground, the King knocked on the door. Edora responded with a "Yes. Come in."

King Beon unlocked the door and brought in the food tray for Edora's meal. He had requested Edora's favorite: bisque soup with fresh, warmed rolls. To not arouse the cook's suspicion, he was ordering a bit more food for himself, not eating all of it, and saving the rest for Edora. Walking in and setting the tray down on the table at the side of the wall that functioned as a dining table and study center, he saw Edora's oracular tools sitting on the corner of the table. They had not been there the day before. Obviously, she had been doing some reading.

"Hello, Edora. I hope you're not feeling too claustrophobic. I plan to have you in a new residence in the next few days once we have solved a few security issues. I do bring news."

"Really? I do as well. The scrying waters and the omens all point in one direction: there was a man, one man, who is after me. I have seen his face several times in the waters, always surrounded by fire. I have no idea who he is or why he is after me, but he is very dangerous and has many powers. The omens tell me that he will

70

return and assert his revenge again. Did you encounter him during the fire attacks?"

"It seems, Edora, we made a narrow escape of him ourselves. By my calculations I removed you from the tower just a few minutes before he had somehow gained access through ill-gotten keys and the answers to the riddles. We have not yet ascertained how, though it would seem Havorth is involved."

"Havorth? No, he wouldn't!"

"Well, it may have been without his knowledge. You said something interesting just a moment ago—that this man has many powers. Do you think it is possible he could have…"

Here he paused, not sure he wanted to verbalize the possibility that this could be true, even to Edora.

She looked at him quizzically and he continued, "Do you believe someone can transform into something else?"

"Like what?" Edora asked.

"Well, like a bird."

"A bird? What kind of bird?"

"From what the General reported, a castle guard testified that Havorth and a sentry were chasing a large, black, raven-like bird down the castle hall. It escaped and Havorth and the sentry have not been forthcoming, saying only that the intruder eluded them. However, the guard saw no one and nothing else, other than the bird, Havorth, and the sentry." He paused, not sure of what else to say. He saw no explanation for these events. Either the intruder was a man-turned-bird, or the intruder escaped through some other means that rendered him invisible. Both options were ludicrous to him, but without having seen the gifts of his Niamá and Edora firsthand, he would have said their abilities were as implausible as shapeshifting.

Edora looked up and to the right in a dreamy state. She was quiet for several moments, making the good King regret his question. *What was I thinking, asking such things? She will think I've gone mad under all of the stress of the past few days.*

Then she began to speak. Her voice sounded hollowed out and neutral, just like it had when King Beon had asked for her first oracle alongside the rutted road many years ago. "The man is a powerful sorcerer, capable of many things that are beyond your understanding. He was the raven transformed by a powerful incantation. He will return. He must be stopped. You will find him by the kingdom of Travessa. He will return."

The King was never sure whose voice was speaking. Was it Edora's own spirit? An ancestor spirit from the overworld? The Devorah spirits? Edora did not know the answer either, only that she felt the voice came through her from a greater being. What greater being it was, she had never been able to discern. The King made sure not to move a muscle and to speak in slow, soft tones to ask her more questions. Anything abrupt could break the flow of her oracle, he knew. "What is to be done with Havorth?" he inquired gently.

She continued to look up and to the right, her trance continuing: "Havorth is guilty only of trusting his lover. He was chosen as escort. If I have chosen him, you must trust him."

"When will the sorcerer return?"

She paused, her eyes turning even glassier. "He will return before the next full moon. He must be stopped. He will return with more vengeance than before, more prepared than before. More deadly than before."

As soon as this last word had left her mouth, her body stirred, her eyes cleared, and she returned to her conscious self. Never remembering much of what she said during these hypnotic states she could spontaneously enter, the King repeated to Edora what she had answered of his questions.

"Yes, my King—Beon." Edora still had a difficult time saying his name without referencing his title. She respected him and she wanted him to know this, yet she also felt her heart stir when she used his personal name. "This is consistent with what I have seen in the waters. He is already plotting his return.

"Do you know who he is or why he might be after you?"

"No. His face is unfamiliar to me. I cannot say. I see that he knows who I am, but I do not know him. I have searched my memory and can make no connections." She was weary and desperate to help but she had not been given any signs as to who this intruder might be.

"Can you return to your trance and I can ask you when you're in that state? Maybe you will receive information about your connection to him."

"The channel has left me for now and I am tired from the looking and divining. I don't think I'll be able to return to the oracle mind until the morrow. You may ask me again then and see what message comes through me. I will rest and restore my energy and my sight until you call again. You do not need to visit me with dinner tonight. This food will be sufficient, and I know you have much business to attend to before we meet again. I will sleep early and well."

"Thank you, Edora. Your words have restored me again. We will be ready for this sorcerer when he returns. I am glad, too, Havorth is no traitor. Sleep well. I will rejoin you in the morn."

"Goodbye, Beon, my King. I will see you soon." Her eyes were already heavy with sleep. The King could foresee on his own that Edora would eat quickly and retire for the day. She could sleep long and hard after an oracle and she had given several over the past few days. That they were filled with horrors, he was sure, only depleted her gifts more. He nodded, and for a reason he could not explain, approached Edora, kissed her softly on the top of her head and turned to retreat from his hidden underworld to the waiting, vulnerable kingdom above.

Edora watched lazily as he left. She would not sleep that night.

As soon as the King was back in his chambers, the first thing on his agenda was to pay a visit to Havorth to confirm the accuracy of the information. However, knowing Edora's accuracy had been nearly one hundred percent over the course of many years, he was more eager to witness the accuracy confirmed in Havorth's eyes upon the information being relayed to him. With this confirmation, he could turn to more important matters: securing and preparing the kingdom for the next assault.

As he made his way down the halls to Havorth's residence, he pondered what other secrets the world might hold that were beyond him. He had heard of sorcery long ago, in legends, in myths, in children's stories, but he had never assumed it was real, or of any importance to his world. Now, it seemed his entire kingdom was dependent on his overcoming a sorcerer. By what means, he had no ideas—yet.

He approached the guard at Havorth's residence and said, "I will enter."

The guard bowed crisply, then reached for his key, unlocked the door, and opened it for the King to enter. The King walked purposefully through and ordered the guard to relock it. Havorth was across the room at his table still eating the midday meal that had been brought to him after the interrogation with the military. Havorth had not looked up as he had assumed it was the guard retrieving his food stuffs. They barely gave him any time to enjoy a meal—one of the many irritating punishments of house arrest. The firm footsteps and brisk cadence, though, signaled a stronger presence than the guard and Havorth looked up just in time to see the King was nearly at his table.

"My liege! My liege!" Havorth squealed as he bumped the table and nearly knocked it over as he rose in order to bow. "I had no idea I would be benefiting from your company. Please allow me to fetch you some drink. I apologize for my rudeness at not anticipating this event."

"How could you, Havorth? Are you an oracle?" the King asked wryly knowing full well Havorth did not believe in such things. Havorth had never known the purpose of the white lady and even if he had been told, the King knew he would have assumed it was rubbish to throw him off track from the truth, as such things as oracles didn't exist. Any who claimed such things were frauds, charlatans, through and through. He was too wise for that ruse. Havorth had answered him with such words once when the King had asked him what he thought about oracles.

Havorth winced at the question, "Of course not, my liege. I do not tell lies. I do not deceive."

"But you haven't told the whole truth either, have you?" King Beon continued not waiting for Havorth's reply. He knew Havorth would just pile on elaborate apologies with excuses and still not come out with the truth. In this case, the truth meant the crumbling of Havorth's black and white world where law and order, and science and nature were the only sure things. To admit the truth was tantamount to betraying his own mind, something Havorth held far too high in esteem—even higher than the law—to spurn.

"What I have learned is something rather shocking. I dare not believe it is true. I have learned that the intruder is known to be a powerful sorcerer who can shapeshift at will. It was a raven this time and that's why the guard said you and the sentry were chasing a bird down the hall only to have it escape by the guard's incomprehension of what was transpiring. But you knew, Havorth, didn't you? You knew the bird was the intruder. That is the only thing that makes sense of all the evidence."

Havorth still stood before his King, shaking violently with the truth of the words the King was throwing at him like darts. "I...I...I don't know what to say, my liege. A man turning into a bird? Who would believe such rubbish? I hope you have not carried this ludicrous rumor to others. They may think you've gone mad. Mad, I say," he stammered.

"Well, I'll see what the other sentry has to say when I ask him." The King gazed carefully at Havorth. He could see Havorth was doing his best not to betray the truth, not to betray himself, and most of all not to betray his reputation any more than it had already been harmed. Havorth's face—even with all its intelligence—betrayed the truth, though, as it winced every time the King spoke it. And upon mentioning the sentry, the King saw the façade crumble as Havorth turned his back on the King to hide his crimping face—a misdeed a not-in-a-panic Havorth would ever have done. Havorth took three paces and then realizing his error, spun back around in horror.

"Oh, my liege, I am sorry. I am so vexed I forgot the rules of etiquette in your Great Presence. Please forgive me. I do not know what ideas the sentry might have gotten into his head. You know he hit it very hard on the stone step that day. I wonder that he's okay and has recovered if he is spouting nonsense about a man turning into a bird and flying away. Oh, the shame. I am so bereaved of all that has occurred."

"But that's not all, Havorth. You not only saw a man turn into a bird and fly, you knew the man, didn't you? You knew him because he was your lover."

With this one word, "lover," Havorth gasped aloud, body frozen, no longer able to conceal his terror. "Why do you say this, my liege? Why..." his words faded as he stared agape and wide-eyed at his King who had not removed his assessing gaze. How had the King found out this information? Havorth had told no one.

"Do not concern yourself with a confession, Havorth. I also know that you did not willingly or consciously betray the kingdom or the tower's secrets. As I said, the intruder is known to be a powerful man. I do not understand it myself, and have a hard time believing it as well. I am surmising that he may have seduced you for your secrets, and unaware, you gave them to him through an enchantment or whatever it is that sorcerers do. I do not believe you are guilty of being a traitor, just of being too trusting of someone you did not know well."

"My liege!" and with his exclamation, Havorth crumpled to his knees, his hands folded, his head bowed with contrition. "I don't know what to say. I don't know how any of this is possible. I don't understand but thank you. Thank you for seeing that I have been true to you, my kingdom, and my post." He wept for the first time ever in his life.

King Beon was a bit taken back at the genuine emotion of Havorth— it was far from Havorth's typical conduct, but the intensity of it revealed and confirmed Edora's oracle to the King. "You may rise, Havorth. There is nothing to forgive. I can see why you kept the relationship hidden. A man with a man is unusual in today's world, but it was not always so, and you are probably wise in being cautious. But the fault was not realizing that you could be a target. That is your fault, but it is also mine. I never anticipated a treachery by someone without honor, let alone one who can do things I didn't think even possible. To forgive myself is also to forgive you. But let us keep this between us for now. Others, too, will not understand, especially the General. I will assure my military that you are no threat, but because I fear the sorcerer is already preparing for a return assault, I must insist that you stay under house arrest and refrain from scribing duties. He may again be able to use you without your awareness, and I want to prevent that, if at all possible."

"Oh yes, my liege. I do agree. Let us keep this quiet between us. I can assure you I will tell no one. You can imagine now why I did not speak of it, yes?"

"Yes, and perhaps it is best that you didn't, so the military will not suspect *you* of madness. In the meantime, I will be able to throw them off of suspecting you by saying that the intruder was a guest scribe of yours from out of town and had copied your keys and stolen the ledger of riddles and knocks and you had not realized due to a nap he medicinally induced of you."

"But my liege, I must protest. I have no such ledger."

"Yes, but they do not know that and since it has been stolen, for our purposes, its supposed absence will hide the necessary deception for now."

"Oh, of course, my liege. Brilliant. That they will buy. I'm sure of it." Havorth sounded as if he were the one who needed the reassuring.

The King was satisfied that Havorth was a willing accomplice and agreeable to being kept under lock and key. It was one less thing for him to concern himself with at this grave time."

"I'm sorry, my liege, for this intrusion. But is Edora safe? I assume the intruder went up the tower to get her for some reason I cannot fathom, but I have not heard of her or her well-being or whereabouts since the firebombs."

"You need not concern yourself. Edora is safe. That is all I will say for now." King Beon turned and strode quickly toward the door. His next priority was to find the book of royals and determine a next of kin so his line could be saved if not secured before any next assault. Having reached the door, he rapped once. The guard unlocked the door from the outside, opened it, and kept it open with an outstretched arm while the King exited and made his way to the library as the guard re-locked the door behind him.

Chapter Twelve

Back in his encampment, the sorcerer, Dayud, planned his next assault on Devor. He would have to act quickly before they had time to regroup and to track him and his men. He encamped on the outer embankments of the kingdom-city of Travessa. Travessa—the most peaceful city in a largely peaceful region where trade treaties kept war away between neighboring peoples—had lived in peace for too many years. Notably, the Travessians were naïve, unsuspicious, too trusting, well-fed. It was the advantage Dayud needed to secretly build his own rebel army right on their doorstep where not one soul would suspect him of treachery, let alone sorcery.

The kingdom of Devor relied on a river, the Bedoga, for water. It flowed directly through the kingdom-city, under its walls through its west and east sides. Without this water source it was a few days on foot to the next river, many hours on horse, and they would be vulnerable to attack and death. Many miles up north, near Travessa, the Bedoga ran extremely close to another river, the Cressic. It was Dayud's strategy to have his men dig a channel from the Bedoga to the Cressic, several days of hard labor, and dam up the Bedoga, effectively choking off Devor's water supply. His plan would have them focused on resolving this crisis and not minding their borders.

He had learned much about manipulating the elements in his training with the great sorcerer, his master, whom he called the Dragoni— the fire breather. The Dragoni had passed his learnings on to Dayud when Dayud was a young man in need of revenge, in need of tutelage. The lessons and initiations took years—requiring much sacrifice and daring. Dayud mastered the elements of wood and wind in the first two initiations. He mastered fire in the third initiation. It took place in a cave on a bottom slope of a semi-active volcano. In the cave, the Dragoni had spoken only what was required.

"Dayud, you have mastered wood and wind. Wood is the fuel of fire, and wind is fire's friend, spreading it, multiplying it. After this initiation there is only the element of water to master. Water is fire's foe. If you cannot master water, you cannot master all the elements and your sorcery will be strong but without longevity."

"I will master fire and I will master water. I will do whatever it takes to have my revenge."

"Yes, but the one whom you seek to vanquish is of the water element. And she is greater than you."

"I doubt you, Dragoni. I gather you only taunt me to make me try harder. There is no way for me to fail. I must have my revenge."

"First things first, my son. Now you must master fire. Are you ready to try?"

"I am ready to succeed."

"Kneel."

Dayud knelt before his Master and bowed his head. Shirtless in the sweltering heat of the sulfuric volcano, he did not know what was coming, but he knew it would be the most difficult initiation he had experienced so far.

The Dragoni took his blade from the stone on which he had just sharpened its edge. With a quick strike he sliced Dayud's top, right shoulder and waited to see the reaction. There was none. Blood had begun oozing out of the clean slit. It ran in rivulets down the front of Dayud, but still he knelt with head bowed. No tears flowed from his closed eyes. The Dragoni took his blade and made another strike, this time on the left shoulder. Still Dayud had not moved a muscle or made a sound. He gave no indication of pain or suffering.

Then from behind the stone that the sword had been lying on, the Dragoni took a bowl fashioned from stone. Within it he had placed some molten lava from a small crevice in the volcano's vent. He had scooped it up from a distance with a long stick carved from stone with a ladle on the end. Even after letting it cool sufficiently, the lava was still hot enough to burn flesh. He poured it slowly on the wound on Dayud's right shoulder. Dayud screamed, writhed, and fell over.

Dayud heard himself screaming. It seemed he was not himself and then he was out of his body.

From this vantage point, he could see everything. He was above his body watching it writhe, hearing his screams but detached somehow from the pain, watching his Master observe him. Was this his spirit? Was this his freedom? His Master then looked up at him in the sky. Did he know? Could he see me? He had learned much from the old man, but he longed to be his own master—to rule the elements himself. He loved and he despised Dragoni. He became aware of more. He was larger than the volcano. He was the volcano. He could feel the power of it melting throughout his being.

A flock of ravens flew by. In an instant they turned toward him. Could they see him, too? As they approached him, one flew off from the conspiracy and into his spirit. He and the raven became one. He flew with the raven—over the mountains, down past a nearby city, whose fertile lands were enriched by the volcanic ash. Then suddenly he/the raven turned and sped back to the volcano, back to the cave, back to his Master. Had his Master called, and he/the bird heard and responded? They flew to his Master who was standing over his still-convulsing human body. His Master held out his arm and they flew to it, landed on it, and stayed waiting. With one word from his Master, the body on the cave floor had stopped its convulsing. He felt disconnected from it as it lay quiet. Was this weary body dead or just unconscious from the pain? He was the bird, too. He knew that.

After a few more minutes, his Master grabbed him—the raven—by its feet and shook it. Dayud didn't know what was happening but he was incensed by the sensation of being shook out of this winged being. He didn't want to give up his freedom. He wanted this body. But then the Dragoni commanded, "Out!" and he was out of the bird. The Master released the bird, telling it, "Leave" and away it flew away from him, without him.

He watched the Master very carefully from his awareness that still was not back in his body, and somehow still distantly attached to it. The Dragoni took some bits of bone and ash and mixed them together in the bowl that had held the lava. He poured in some steaming water from a cup heated by another bowl of lava, mixing it together, waving his hands, uttering an incantation below his breath.

All Dayud could make out was, "The fire that burned is the fire that healed. The water shall do as the fire requires."

The Dragoni blew on the potion, then dipped his fingers into the mix and smeared some of it on his own forehead. After doing so, he knelt down beside Dayud's own deathly quiet body and again put his fingers into the concoction. As he smeared some on Dayud's own body's forehead, the Dragoni whispered a few more words Dayud couldn't quite make out.

In an instant, Dayud was back in his body. His shoulders throbbed. He couldn't move. He couldn't even open his eyes. He could think, though. He could feel. His body wasn't dead. But, oh, how heavy he felt after experiencing the freedom of flight. How burdened he was with all that his memories carried in his body. How he dreaded the tasks that lay before him.

After a few more words he could hear his Master saying over him, he fell into a deep sleep. In the morning, he slowly sat up. Had he dreamed he was a bird? A raven? He didn't see his Master anywhere. There was a plate of figs and bread left for him. He ate ravenously. When he was done, he noticed throbbing in his shoulders again. He looked at his right one and saw a big open wound, oozing, pale and sickly-looking. So, it wasn't a dream. It had been real. He looked at his left shoulder and saw that it was already healing.

He got up slowly, still weak from the pain his body had been through the night before. Where was his Master?

Almost before he had finished this thought, the Dragoni appeared from around the corner of the cave. He had some weeds in his hand.

He nodded at Dayud but said nothing. Picking up another stone bowl, he put the weeds into it, and with a rock, pounded them. He then spit into the bowl and said yet another incantation below his breath. With his fingers he smeared the salve into Dayud's right shoulder. It seared almost as much as the lava, but somehow, he was able to detach from within his body. He could manage the pain this time.

Dayud sat down slowly and drank some water the Dragoni had fetched him from a cup elsewhere in the cave.

"So," Dragoni announced, "You have passed the fire initiation. You defeated fire with air-wind-spirit. You did not master it with water, which is your weakness. It is well for you that a conspiracy of ravens happened by so you could learn to fly. Do not think you have mastered the form yet. The raven mastered you. Until you can become the raven in your own body, you will be a mediocre sorcerer. You have much to learn."

Dayud could feel his internal fires again raging as they had for many years. He would master the raven, he would master the water, and then he would master the Dragoni.

After the fire initiation, in the weeks, months, and years that followed, the Dragoni taught Dayud how to master form and shapeshift into an old man, like Dragoni and into a raven. He could only shapeshift into that which had first mastered him. After learning form, he was ready to master the element of water.

They camped near a creek where Dayud would undergo the water initiation. On the morning of the initiation, Dayud found the Dragoni asleep beside the creek. Dayud was puzzled. The Dragoni never slept late. He bent down to shake and rouse him from his slumber but the Dragoni never roused. He was dead. Dayud never received the water initiation, for the Dragoni had left him.

After burying his Master's body beside the creek he retreated a few days ride to the Dragoni's shack in the woods. There he studied the texts and incantations his Master had written down but had never shared with Dayud. Now Dayud knew everything the Dragoni did. A water initiation didn't matter when he knew all the secrets of his Master.

And so, it was many years later, that he set out with his men who had regathered with him after the firebombs on Devor. They decamped from Travessa and traveled to where the banks of the Bedoga and Cressic rivers nearly wed, in order to master Devor.

Chapter Thirteen

After Edora heard the King lock the door behind him, she quickly got up and started packing essentials: her divining tools, some food she had been stashing, as well as a water bag and extra clothing. She intended to leave that night. She had been pondering it since the day before when she had seen in the waters that the man who attacked Devor had for some reason come for her and was planning to return. Soon after that revealing scry, she'd dropped a utensil off the side of the bed. The metal-forged spoon had made a hollow clunk on what was supposedly a dirt floor. Sweeping the dirt away, a brick appeared. When she picked up the brick, a key dropped out of it. She tried it in the door, and it unlocked. Edora realized this must be the King's hidden key in case he had lost his other key or if he had been forced here by an enemy, so he had a means of escape.

After hearing Beon's words that the sorcerer had escaped by turning himself into a raven, she decided that she must leave as soon as possible. That was the only way he would be stopped. If he was that powerful, Devor didn't stand a chance. And if she was what he was after, then she must leave and save Devor. She couldn't be the reason that more people died, more land destroyed, and possibly the King himself killed. He meant more to her than anyone. She couldn't bear the thought of his death. She had seen too much of that in her life. She was not going to be the cause of any more destruction.

When she had packed the essentials, she rested to reserve her energy for her evening's escape. As soon as dusk had begun to settle, when she determined the King was probably at his evening meal, she took the key, unlocked the door as quietly as she was able, and hurried up the stairs as softly as her leather-soled feet would carry her.

At the top of the stairs was another locked door. Edora hadn't anticipated this. She hoped the key to the bottom door also unlocked this door.

Putting the key into the lock, she turned it slowly to loosen any sound from hastening. It clicked and turned. *What a relief,* she thought to

85

herself. *Now, to make my way out of the King's chamber and out of the castle without being noticed.*

She looked around at what was clearly his bedroom. The room smelled of his musky scent, a familiar comfort, and enticed her to stay—to remain with Beon and Devor and never leave. She shook her head, trying to clear the pull of the heady allure from her senses. After regaining herself, she tip-toed hurriedly through the room and peeked beyond another door to what she guessed must be his private study with book-lined walls, ornately wooden shelves and lacquered floors. After not seeing anyone in there, she ran through to the far door—she concluded it must be the way out.

Opening this door quietly as a whisper and grateful the King's quarters were well kept—especially the oiled door locks and hinges—she slipped into an intermediary room that would be for the King's attendants. None were there. Fortune and the spirits were on her side.

As she was passing through this room, Edora spied a blanketing wrap made up of some kind of gray threads. *That would be perfect for a traveling cloak,* she surmised, and she lifted it from its hook and threw it around her. *All the better to hide my white linen dress and skin.* As she continued through the attendants' room, she caught sight of herself in some type of looking glass. It was the clearest looking glass she had ever beheld. The only looking glasses she had ever seen were water and a pounded metal substance she didn't know the name of. She reached out her hand to touch it. Marble cold and jewel hard, she thought to herself, *Perhaps I can see images from the spirit world in this.*

She stood for a moment in front of the mirror and then brushed the thought away quickly. *I don't have time for this.* Then, just as she was turning, she saw a small wooden frame with a similar looking glass within it. She picked it up and looked at her white reflection looking clearly back at her, the gray cloak draped over her. She was still an orphan girl.

Startled to realize she had dallied yet again, she stuffed the small looking glass into her bag and made her passage swiftly to the other side of the room. As she did, she spied a side door. *It must be how attendants enter the King's chambers directly without going through the main entrance.* She tried the door, but it was locked. Fairly sure the stolen key would not work, she tried it anyway and was not terribly surprised to find she was unable to make the connection.

Panic started to rise as she knew the next passage would take her into the main section of the King's residence where she would find the dinner table, kitchens, and entry to the elaborate public court where the King's wise presence presided monthly. Many people would be in these areas. Before the King had hidden her away in the tower years ago, he had given her a quick tour of the castle which she remembered as if it were yesterday. She had often imagined what her life would be like if she were able to traverse these grand rooms, if she had free reign of the castle grounds, and all of this were normal. She had not long-dwelt on these images as she dismissed them as the fantasies of a former pauper and an orphan girl.

Just as Edora was about to risk stepping out of the attendants' room and into the dining areas, a maid stepped in from the locked side door. "Oh!" the maid exclaimed as she almost ran square into Edora. "What are you doing here?"

Edora stared back at her, wide-eyed. "I was…"

"Oh, that's right. You must be the new cook I was told about. Sorry for the scare. I had forgotten you would be showing up. You're a little late. Dinner's already begun." The maid eyed Edora carefully, still unsure of this odd-looking creature.

"I got lost. It's my first time in the castle proper. A doorman showed me in, but I'm not knowing what to do." Edora breathed a silent sigh. She hoped her heart's racing was just as silent.

"Yes, yes, well, here is your closet." She pointed to the cupboard door next to last on the left-hand side. "You'll find your uniform in there and you can take it into this dressing room that is just for the women." Here, she pointed to adjoining doors with little hallways that led off the main seating area. "You may leave your bag and any personal items in your cupboard. They will be secure."

"Thank you, ma'am." Edora curtsied.

"Just hurry up, and when you're readied, take this hall down to the kitchens and I'll meet you there for your first assignment."

"Yes, ma'am. Thank you, ma'am."

The maid nodded and went and fetched something from a side pantry with linens folded neatly inside, and then turned and sped off.

Edora couldn't believe this. Her mamá and papá must be looking out for her!

She quickly opened the cupboard door, picked up the neatly folded uniform off the bottom of the shelf along with some sturdy, soled slippers, and darted off to change quickly in the dressing room.

Emerging from the dressing room in her cook uniform, she stuffed her new wrap into her bag and headed out in the opposite direction of her instructions, directly to the main exit that led to the dining and kitchen areas. She turned right at the first side hallway, hoping it would lead to other side hallways that ended at an outside door.

After several more turns, she thought, *This castle is a maze. Probably intentionally so for anyone like me, who wasn't supposed to be there could be discovered before finding their way out.*

As she made her way around yet another turn, she almost ran headlong into the doorman keeping a door to the outside safe from the inside.

"Whoa, miss. What are you doing over here? Shouldn't you be down in the kitchens?"

"Oh, I'm new and I'm lost. I was just leaving and couldn't find my way out to get home to my mamá. Could you let me out, kind sir?"

"Why didn't you use the servants' quarters door?"

"They haven't given me a key yet, and I was off and need to get home and all of the servants were still busy serving dinner. Rather than wait I decided to find my way out by myself, and here I am. I'm so sorry if this inconveniences you."

"Not at all, miss. Make sure they give you that key, tomorrow," the doorman moved his hand as if to dismiss her apology.

"Of course, I will. Thank you again. I must hurry home to my poor mamá before it gets dark."

"Keep safe, then, for your mamá's sake," and he opened the door wide for her.

Edora curtsied as she made her way through and ignored the guard on the outside of the door as he suspiciously spied her odd and sudden appearance through a door seldom used by the servants.

As she hurried down the cobblestone street, she overheard the doorman explain to the guard why she had used that door, but turning a corner she was then out-of-sight, and also out of earshot.

After making it down a good measure of the road that led to the outer gates, she hid in a corner that during the day was used as a street market. There she pulled out the cloak, wrapped it around her so the uniform was fully hidden, and reached inside her bag for the next item she was going to need to make it out of Devor.

The light was fading nearly as quickly as snuffing out a candle and she quickened her pace to make it to the kingdom gates before they were locked for the night—at total darkness. Even at dusk they were closed and only by a special order could anyone be let in or out.

In a few minutes, she had made it to the gates. Dark was near and she did not know if she had made it in time. She would find out soon enough.

She stepped up to the guard at the gate booth built into the kingdom wall but unlike the outer gate booth, it was situated on the ground. "Dear sir, I am late leaving my castle duties to make it to my mamá's house that sits on the outside of the walls near the river. She is expecting me, and I hope to bring her some food that she relies on."

"Not without a special order of the King or other ranking official, I cannot. These are dangerous times."

"Oh, of course, I forgot. Forgive me. Here is a release from the King himself."

Edora held out the sealed envelope she had taken from her bag when she pulled the cloak out and covered her uniform.

The guard took the envelope and saw the King's wax stamp on the outside. He looked up and sized her appearance and said, "Why would the King sign an order for you? What is your job in the castle?"

"Oh, I am a scullery maid in the kitchens." Here, Edora let part of her cloak drop to reveal the cook uniform beneath. "My mamá was a friend of the King's cousin so that is how I got the job and how I came to inquire that the King allow me to visit my mamá, now that her friend, the King's cousin, is dead."

He scowled at her impudence. A scullery maid on speaking terms with the King? This King was too friendly with the servants. Nevertheless, he broke open the seal to find a letter written in the King's longhand including his signature and stamp granting Edora permission to exit the kingdom grounds before nightfall.

"Well, then, since nightfall is imminent, I better let you go through at once, otherwise I'll be breaking the law." He thought better of letting her go through even now, but not wanting to disturb a superior after nightfall, he opened a small gate inside the larger kingdom gate for individuals to go through. "Hurry off, then. Get to your mamá's as quick as you can."

"Thank you, I will! And thank you from my mamá!"

Edora scurried through the door and headed to the left and north towards the river. After he watched her run off into the night, he closed the gate, secured it, and noted the passage in the log, muttering under his breath again about the laxity of the King.

Oh, mamá! Edora thought as loudly as she could in her head. *Thank you for assisting me. I'm so sorry about all the deception I had to tell to get out, but it's the only way to save these dear people and the King.*

After she knew she would be out of sight, she ran as fast as she could to the river. It would take her north, which is where she had divined the sorcerer to be. She had no light, but her senses were keen and the moon was on its way to being full and bright. The river was just ahead of her and the moon's reflection on the water would be enough to guide her, she was sure of it.

She slowed as she neared some of the outer homes clustered by the river. She didn't want to be heard or seen. The cloak made her next to invisible and kept her warm in the cooling night air. She could still smell the burnt wood up ahead of her. Alas, all of those beautiful trees lost! She had often admired their beauty from her tower afar. She imagined the tree faeries her mamá told her about. She had never seen them, but her mamá could and would describe their pretty colors and fanciful dances amidst the flowers and trees of their home, before they had to flee for their lives. Edora wondered what had happened to the tree faeries of the forest. Did they flee like her and her mamá had to, or die like her papá chose to?

Edora whispered a prayer to the spirits into the night for safe keeping. Trusting that most of the wild animals had run off from the fire, she made her way to the riverbank and looked down at the dark, moving, looking glass. It would not reveal any secrets. That would have to wait. She talked to the river spirit, asking her to wind her way to the north with speed and safety.

Chapter Fourteen

As she walked along in silence, she approached the still-steaming remains of the forest that touched the river. The ashy trunks looked like ghosts standing tall in a charcoal cemetery. The air was still and as smoky as an old trader's tavern, so she covered her face with her cloak and tried to breathe with the filter of its natural fiber. To cover her fear, she began to hum. Songs her mamá had sung to her long ago, that she had forgotten over time, returned to her in this night and she hummed them all as a lullaby to herself.

She had almost reached the far side of the burned-out forest when she heard a rustling sound to her right. The river was still to her left. If she had to, she could hide beneath an overhang in the bank. She peered carefully over her right shoulder but saw nothing. An owl hooted its mourn for the loss of its home overhead, sending Edora jumping at the fright.

She continued on, silently again, not wanting any sounds to give her away and lead to an attack. Every so often she would sense someone or something following her and would turn and look but could still see nothing. What good was second sight, if it didn't reveal a threat?

Again, she heard a rustling and decided to take cover. Running down to the river, along the shallow bank she found an overhang that would hide her sufficiently from human eyes—though she doubted an animal out at night would be fooled by this. Her smell alone could be tracked and anything nocturnal would also have keen sight in this moonful darkness.

Edora tightly pulled the cloak around her and pressed herself even further into the concave-shaped alcove in the bank. What or who could be following her? No one at the castle had known she was gone and if they were looking for her, wouldn't they be calling out, not lurking behind her?

Was the sorcerer about? A bear exiled by the fire? She noticed her body was trembling. Was it from fear or the cold or from sheer exhaustion? *Maybe all*, she thought to herself. The night grew a little darker as a cloud passed in front of the moon. Frogs and crickets that had survived the fire began their croaking and creaking. She didn't hear any more rustling. No footsteps. Nothing but the creatures that serenaded her.

After many more minutes of waiting that felt like hours, she had to decide. Would she risk getting up again or stay here and rest for an odd hour or two before continuing her journey? Her body was aching to stay. She willed it to get up and try again. She could always hide again if necessary.

Pulling herself up, she stretched out of the overhang with her cloak still snugly wrapped around her. Turning to her left, in the steady direction of north, she was just about to begin walking when something from behind her, pushed her—hard. Screaming, she jumped forward and spun around. She could see a large, dark, shadowy shape in front of her, but with the moonlight obscured, she didn't know what it was. It wasn't attacking, so she determined to stand still.

Holding in her fear was like holding back a flood with a papery dam. She stared at the looming figure. It must be looking back at her, too, studying her, waiting to attack, maybe. Suddenly, the large shadow snorted and neighed. She fell back from the fright but upon landing began laughing. She couldn't stop. It had been so long since she had laughed. Soon, she was in tears. Then, the wisp of a dam broke. All the remembered rivers of sorrow merged into a mighty torrent of grief and she let them all flow. The horse was her friend, her protector, here to guide her to safety. She was sure of it. But this beast had come as the fearful shadow of an enemy to scare her to her core where all the emotions of years had been wrapped up tighter than her cloak with nothing stronger than a tissue.

When the grief had subsided, she felt like the turbulence of a thunderstorm had swept through her entire being and now all was calm. She wiped her tears on the cloak and stood to assess the mighty beast. She put out her hand and he nuzzled it. She thought it was a he, anyway. Guessing he was hungry, she reached in her bag and found an apple and brought it out for him. He eagerly snacked on it, and then walked up beside her where she could pet his mane. And, oh, he was no wild horse. His saddle was still on him, a bit askance. She figured he must be a military horse that had escaped in the fireball attack and been wandering ever since.

"Hi there, fella. We've found each other now. I need to ride north. Would you carry me, and we'll go together?"

The horse moved his neck back to whinny and she saw in her mind's eye the horse running with her on it, so she took that as the horse's answer. Finding the cinch to the saddle by feeling around with her hands, she straightened and tightened it and then made way to swing up with her left foot in the stirrup. It took a few tries. She was diminutive and he was not.

After getting up atop him, she felt safe at last. "I will name you, christen you, Saza, for saving me. Let's be off," and she signaled with the reins and gave a little nudge into his belly as she had seen riders do. As he was clearly well-trained, he was off and climbing the bank, and up and beside it in a few paces.

Several hours later when the dark night had grown into a shadowy figure, Edora could no longer keep her eyes open. She pulled on the reins and Saza halted. She could tell he needed rest too, so she jumped off and led him down to the riverbank much farther north than when they had first met and allowed him to drink his delight. She found another apple and some root vegetables, and he ate them heartily. She snacked on some bread then drank from her water pouch. Edora tied the reins to her bag, which she then laid on so Saza would not wander off. He must have sensed her need to rest and he did not tug or pull, and she fell into a deep sleep very quickly. It was so deep she didn't dream.

She awoke with a start. A blinding pain pierced her eyes. *What is that?*

Oh, it's only the sun. Considering the low rise of the burgeoning star over the eastern horizon, it was still very early in the morning. Saza had taken to resting as well and was asleep beside her. Upon standing and stretching and looking around, Edora's movements awoke Saza, and he stretched up into standing after a couple of arthritic tries. In the daylight, she could see that his coat was a shimmery gold—she had never before seen such a magickal-looking beast. After leading him down to the water again to let him drink, she spoke out loud (she was glad to use her voice). "The first thing we do is get you some food. Let's follow the river some more. I believe there must be a village along here somewhere." She took a few moments and changed out of her stolen maid uniform, which she hoped to be able to return some day, and put on her white linen dress. It would be odd and invite too many questions to have a maid show up at a village on a military horse.

She ran him a bit to get the morning stiffness out of his legs, his gait surer and surer as he galloped. Clouds were beginning to gather in the south. Rain might arrive by nightfall. She felt it in the air. "Good," she said out loud to Saza who whinnied back. "We need more rain after such a long dry winter."

A small low-lying range up ahead looked like a good place for a village to nestle itself in the valley, like the peoples around here preferred. They raced to the first hill and then slowly walked their way up. It was good to see trees again, not at all plentiful like the former forest at Devor, but the few trees brought birds and life and hope.

At the crest of the first hill, Edora halted Saza to assess their location. They were higher than any of the other hills, and she could see a remarkable distance. There was indeed a tiny village in a nook beside the river over a small rise up ahead. She paused to let Saza graze on some grass that he had started to nibble under his feet.

When he looked up, she took the opportunity to lead him forward, and reluctantly, it seemed, he started off down the hill. "When we get to the village, there will be food for you there. I promise, Saza." He snorted but kept right on ahead, as if determined to reach the village before any food might run out by means of any interlopers.

As they started their way down the hill, a trail appeared ahead. *It must be a village trail used to scout the area*, thought Edora. Rocky, with sparse vegetation, the hillside would have made for an unsure descent without the well-worn trail. Saza, strong-footed, made the way down easily enough. With the rhythm of his gait, Edora was lulled into a contemplative state and she mulled over her escape. *The King will not have found that I am missing yet. His discovery will still be a couple of hours away. I hope to be on the other side of this village and range by then, but I will need to find some type of shelter that will conceal us if I divine the King's search party is near.*

She hoped she would be able to find the sorcerer and stave off whatever his plans were to attack Devor again. *What kind of mind intends destruction? From whence did his powers arise?* These types of questions were running through her thoughts just as the village appeared over the small hill she had seen from above. Edora was sure the sorcerer was not here. The energy of the little village was clear and bright with an aura of a shimmering, rosy hue.

The trail made its way directly to the village. Saza, upon seeing the homes, perked up, sensing food was nearby, and his gait quickened an almost imperceptible amount. Within a few minutes they had arrived at what appeared to be the village center. It opened in a large half-circle next to the river with several still-not-open-for-trading shops lining the arcing layout. Dismounting, Edora led Saza down to the river for some water and then led him back to the town center where she had spotted some hay in a trough left by a shop owner for feed for the customer's horses.

While Saza ate contentedly, Edora sat down beside him and pulled out some bread and cheese for her breakfast. Looking at her food reserves, she guessed she had about one, maybe two, days' worth left. Her divining had said she needed up to three days' worth of food. Saza had eaten some of that, so she hoped she'd find the sorcerer soon since with Saza she was making much better time— although the divining might have anticipated that even when she didn't. Well, maybe at a future village, she could trade something for some food if needed. She had no idea what she had that might be worth anything. She wanted to do some more divining but didn't want to risk it here where villagers and shop owners might soon be showing up. Saza seemed to finish about the time that she did, so she led him back to the river for another drink and then went back to a hand pump near the village center and refilled her water pouch. She hoped to repay these villagers for the hay and water when she had the chance in the future.

She mounted Saza, the first try this time, and off they walked out of the still-dreaming village. They were up and over the next hill when, suddenly, Saza tripped and stumbled. Edora nearly fell off of him but when it was clear Saza was not okay, she dismounted quickly, not wanting to cause any added weight to an injury.

"Oh no, dear Saza, whatever has happened?" She looked behind them at the trail and a big rock had apparently been the culprit. Saza whinnied and jumped every time he tried to put his right front hoof down. Edora went to his right side and talked gently to him. "It's okay, Saza. I'm not going to hurt you. I just need to feel your leg and see what's wrong. Will you let me do that?" Since she believed Saza had sent her a picture in her mind to answer her question once, she tried to do the same, sending him a clear picture of what she wanted to do.

Saza settled a little, which she took as a yes, so Edora started to feel up and down the injury. Right below the knee, Saza pulled his leg when she touched there. It was hot. He wouldn't let her touch it any more firmly, so she didn't know if it was broken or just sprained. Either way, they would not be going anywhere. She couldn't just leave him there and getting him back to the village was impossible, too.

She continued to speak soothingly to him caressing his leg above the injury and then a picture popped into her mind. Once when she was a little girl and she was running around with some of the other village children, she had put her foot into a little hole and twisted her ankle as she fell. The children had run back to her house and told her mamá that she was hurt. When her dear mamá made it back to her, she dried Edora's tears with her apron and said, "There, there, Edora, my love. Not to worry, it will be better very soon." Then her mamá had blown on her ankle. The pain was gone! After that her mamá had laid her hands on Edora's ankle, it had gotten really hot, but it felt good, like the warmth of a summer sun after a cold rain. When her mamá was finished, Edora had gotten back up and could run around with the children again like she had never been hurt.

Edora didn't have all the gifts her mamá had, but she had gifts her mamá never had either. She didn't know if this would work or not, especially on a horse, but she had to try.

"Okay, Saza, I'm first going to blow on your leg and then I'm going to touch it again to try and heal it. Is that okay?"

Saza whinnied and settled his leg so she again took this as a yes. Edora went inside like she did before an oracle or a divining. She whispered a "help" to the Devorah and the spirits around her. Then she imagined a white, brilliant light and she blew on Saza's injury. She blew and blew just like her mamá had and more, hoping that more was better. She could sense Saza was accepting what she was doing, but she had no idea if it was working. She continued blowing just to give it as much as she could and stopped when she was winded. Then she said to Saza, "Okay, I'm going to put my hands on your leg now. I hope this heals and doesn't hurt."

Saza stayed still so she wrapped her hands around his leg and said some concocted words of an incantation about healing. Saza didn't protest this time. Then she waited. After a few seconds her whole body felt warm like she was standing under a tropical waterfall. Her hands started to get very hot, so she kept them firm against his leg until she felt the heat leave her hands.

Pulling her hands away, she said out loud, "Well, Saza, that's all I can do. How do you feel?"

Saza whinnied again and jumped. He came down square on both his front legs and didn't pull up at all on his right leg. It worked!

Still not wanting to risk it, she led Saza slowly a ways to test if it was going to give him any more problems. It seemed to be fine, and so she mounted him and took it gently up and over the rest of the small hills to the flat plains beyond. She thought she could make out a large city in the far distance, but it really was too far to tell. She hoped it was Travessa, the city she hazily remembered the King telling her about after her trance and channeling.

By mid-morning, she and Saza were both ready for a break. They had continued following the river, as she had divined it would take her north to the sorcerer. After snacking at the riverside, Edora decided now was a good time to do some more divining. She ruffled through her bag and found the framed looking glass she had taken from the servants' closet in the castle. She didn't know if it would show her any images or not. If not, she would use the river, but she wanted to try.

She got quiet inside where not even a whisper could stir and looked deeply into the mirror. Unlike using water as a looking glass, the mirror was still, without the movement to naturally make images from itself. She unfocused her eyes a little more and allowed there to be whatever would be. Her vision went blank as if a cloud had just moved between her and the mirror. Then images burst onto the blank screen in front of her. Fire, fire, flames, and more flames, and she saw herself screaming. The images morphed into all sorts of disturbing images. She became more and more absorbed with everything she was seeing as if she herself were experiencing it. Suddenly, she became aware that she was screaming in the here and now just as she dropped the looking glass—and right before it shattered on a riverbank rock—she saw the face of King Beon looking back at her in shock. She knew—he had just discovered her missing.

Chapter Fifteen

King Beon had gone down to Edora's hiding place in the late morning—the time when she preferred to eat a brunch-like breakfast. After knocking on the door and not hearing anything, he unlocked it and spoke into the door crack, "Edora? Edora! I'm here with some food. Are you still in bed?"

Not hearing anything again, he opened the door a little further and spoke into the room a bit louder. "Edora! It's the King. Are you not well?"

The silence echoed back at him ominously, and he quickly walked in and set the food tray down on the multi-use table. He checked behind every piece of furniture in the room. He then walked into the only other room she could possibly be in, the bedroom, and saw no one. Now in a panic, he searched as if she might have been a child thinking that hide-and-seek would be a fun game. He looked under the bed, in the closets, even behind the door he had first come through, but she was gone. *How could she have gotten out? Did the sorcerer find her and magick her out in some way of escape?*

Then a thought entered his mind, *The key!* He raced back to the bedroom and looked for the buried brick. There it was, looking like it had recently been dusted. He pulled it out of its hole and sure enough, the key was missing and in its place was a letter. The King took it out, unfolded it, and read it quickly:

Dear King Beon,

I am so sorry to have caused you worry when you did not find me. I am guessing that this is late morning and you have come to bring me my breakfast. Please know I am doing this for the best of everyone. The sorcerer wants me and so by taking my leave of Devor, I can save you all from more destruction and death. I do not want to be the reason any more people suffer or any more of the earth is scorched. Do not come after me. It will be of no use. You will not find me. I hope to return to you and Devor someday, but I do not know if or when. No one else is responsible for my escape except me.

Yours in service,

Edora

The King stood in shock for a moment and then suddenly snapped to, when he thought he saw an image of Edora screaming beside a river flash in his mind. *Maybe she's following the river north to Travessa, exactly where she had oracled the sorcerer was. Why is she doing such a foolish thing? Doesn't she understand that someone like the sorcerer has no honor and giving herself up to him would not stop him from attacking Devor if he had it within his heart to do so? He might do it just for the thrill of it—just to prove his powers. Edora may have the wisdom of Spirit, but she is naive in the ways of dishonorable men.*

Fortunately, the next assembly with the military was about to begin. He could order a search party for her immediately. In the meantime, he had an errand for one of his footmen to run. After securing the safe house below, he found a footman in the servants' quarters. The footman was eager to fulfill the duty the King whispered to him and set off immediately while the King set off in the opposite direction for the Great Room, taking the halls at twice the speed of his usual pace.

While Edora picked up what large pieces of the broken mirror she could salvage, she wondered why she'd started screaming. The images were not that different from anything she had seen in the past while scrying. She still had no understanding of what they meant, except that now they were even more troubling. She had hoped the images would have changed—that now that she had left Devor, she had averted some of the future disasters she had foreseen—and the images would have at least faded or be less troubling. Instead they seemed stronger, even closer to her in time.

She wrapped the jagged edges of the magick mirror carefully in clothes she had in her bag so she wouldn't cut herself on them the next time she needed to scry. Now that the King had found her missing, she was fairly certain he would send out a search party to come looking for her, even though she had told him not to do so. She was ahead of them by over half a day and hoped that would be enough to stay ahead of them. She at least had the advantage that the King did not know for certain where she had gone. Nevertheless, tonight she would need to find someplace more secure to rest. She could not risk upending her plan. After drinking some water from her pouch, she put it back in her bag and threw the bag over her shoulders and mounted Saza.

Saza's leg had not seemed to give him any more problems, but she didn't want to risk running him yet. So, they traveled at a steady gait through the next few hours under the winter sun—even at high noon it was low on the horizon. The clouds continued to gather and darken, chilling any warmth the sun's rays could get through to her still waiflike body. She was nearly thirty-three but was often mistaken for an older girl.

The plains were long and dull. Saza was wearying from the long hours and her body was beginning to ache from the strain of continually sitting astride a horse after sleeping on the ground in the early morning hours. She may have to call it a night at dinner. If only she could find some place to rest that wasn't so out in the open!

The sun started to arch its way closer to its western berth. With the drop in temperature, the clouds felt it was their time to drop their moisture and soon a misting had begun to fall with Edora having little to keep her dry except the cloak. She pulled it out of her bag and wrapped it tightly around her and over her head. When the mist turned to a light rain, she signaled to Saza to increase his gait, which he seemed glad to do. His trot was as sure-footed as before his injury. Edora thanked the Devorah and her spirits again for helping her heal his leg.

The terrain started to slope downward. She had not seen this geographical feature from afar as it dipped below her line of sight on the plains. The sloping revealed another village nestled in a narrow valley between the extension of plains on either side. It was much too small to be the big city of Travessa, but larger than the last village so she could perhaps spend the night here. There were trees for cover from the rain with many more houses and shops than the last stop making it possible for there to be a guest cottage or some type of place to rest for the night out of the elements.

Upon seeing the village, himself, Saza increased to a cantor, but Edora didn't allow him to run into a full gallop—still not wanting to press her luck with his leg. As they neared, it appeared some of the shops were yet open for trade at the latening hour. The village square was situated a bit up from the river, and sat near the center of the community, with homes spreading out like a fan from it. Quaint, and looking better off than the last village, Edora wished for the best. Riding Saza right into the middle of town—with dusk near—she drew all the shop owners' and shoppers' attentions. *Not exactly hiding myself here, am I?* she thought to herself. But the approaching weather and nearing darkness had changed her mind about trying to shelter herself in some wayward, makeshift lean-to where no one would notice her.

Edora halted Saza at the village square and dismounted. She stretched her legs to relieve the stiffness that had settled after such a long ride. Her body was not accustomed to the rigors of life atop an animal. She turned and saw an old man approaching her.

"My dear, my dear, why are you out in this weather?" He looked up quizzically at her with a sparkle in his eye, "Oh, never mind, never mind. I have been waiting for you. I have food for you and your horsey, and shelter, too! Follow me!" And he turned around and started walking off in a direction away from the river.

Edora didn't know what to think or what to do. *Should she trust this old man? He had been waiting for her? What did he mean?*

"Excuse me, kind sir."

"Yes?" the old man turned around and looked at her with apparent surprise that she was not already following him. He came back a few steps closer.

"What village is this? I am on a long journey and though I am on the right road I am not quite sure where I am right now." Edora wanted to make sure this wasn't Travessa, for if it were Travessa, maybe this man was the sorcerer and that's how he had known she was coming. She wasn't mentally prepared to turn herself into him yet.

"Oh, my dear, this is the village of Javenia. I thought you knew that?"

"Er, no." *Knew that? Had this old man confused her with someone else? Or was he perhaps senile?* Edora looked around at the other villagers to see if they gave any indication that this exchange was odd or dangerous, but she noted that they had all returned to their business at hand and were ignoring her and the old man completely.

The old man turned back and around and waved his hand, "Come. Follow me."

Saza decided to start following the old man all on his own as if he knew this would be the fastest way to get food and rest. Edora said a silent prayer for protection and allowed Saza to lead the way this time.

"No need for that, my dear! You should be thanking me instead," the old man shouted back at her as if he had just read her mind, and then he chuckled.

Feeling less and less secure, Edora nevertheless trusted the villagers. They seemed good-hearted. *They wouldn't let a traveling waif and her horse go off to their doom without saying a word, would they?*

And so, Edora and Saza walked on behind the old man, totally unprepared for what was about to happen next.

King Beon arrived at the Great Room and motioned to his General to join him in the corner of the room where the King spoke to him in hushed tones. When they were through, they made their way to the council table and General Morlay called those who had already assembled to order.

"Men of Devor: We are assembled today to discuss further matters of considerable urgency concerning the security of our great kingdom-city. Yesterday, we heard from the former scribe, Havorth, and today we were to decide his guilt or innocence. The King and I have just conferred, and he has informed me that a secret envoy of his has determined that although Havorth's keys were the ones copied, Havorth himself is guilty only of bringing into his acquaintance a man totally untrustworthy and giving him access to his private quarters. Of greater importance, the King also tells me, is that this special envoy of his is now missing and Havorth is at grave risk of once again coming under the same unsavory man's influence. The King would like to address you directly and so please, stand for your King, Beon."

The King stood as did the rest of the council and then he motioned for them to sit again. When the screeching of wood on tile had stopped, the King surprised them all with his speech:

"I am going to tell you something I have never told anyone. For years I have kept it secret and by doing so I have protected many people and this kingdom. However, it is now in the best interest of the kingdom that the secret is revealed to you. The white lady is an oracle. My Niamá was an oracle. For many of the years I have served as your King I have used the gifts of these women to rule peacefully. You could say they have been my secret weapon. You may not want to believe in such things. I am not here to persuade you otherwise. Yet, it is your duty to protect this kingdom and so we must find the white lady. She has gone missing. I believe it is of her own accord and I also believe she is at the moment not in harm's way. But she, I believe, may be walking into a trap that might kill her or put the kingdom at even greater risk than if she were here.

"You must understand that somehow the men that attacked us found out about the oracle, even though I had told no one. Perhaps Havorth said something to our attacker—off-hand—that tipped him off that he was the keeper of an oracle, though Havorth himself knows not what the white lady is, nor does he believe in such things. Their target was initially to find the oracle and kidnap her. When this failed, as I had already removed her from her tower to a safer location, the attacker's back-up plan was to destroy us and her with the firebombs. They were ready and they did release them when their leader had escaped from the kingdom and had signaled for them to do so. However, our army, having already assembled due to the oracle's foresight, was able to prevail against them, without suffering beyond the few deaths and burnt houses.

"Now the white lady has decided it would be safer for everyone if she were not here and so out of goodness has fled. I am not yet sure of her escape, but I am guessing she may have gone to give herself up to the attacker, in hopes of staving off another attack on Devor by him that she has seen is imminent. She hopes her life will be an exchange for the life of the kingdom. But the white lady, though wise in foresight, has made a hurried error. With her gifts, the attacker could use her against her will to level this kingdom and others to the ground.

"My task today is to implore you to table the decision on the guilt or innocence of Havorth and to send out a scouting party to Travessa in the north to track the last known camp of the attacker. This scouting party must now also become a search party for the white lady, known to me as Edora. Since she is most likely heading in the same direction as a scouting party would go anyway, no time will be lost. I am only asking for more attention to scouting to seek her on the given route. It is of the utmost importance that we retrieve her before he does. Time is of the essence. Though I have revealed this secret to you today, you are sworn to secrecy as a military oath. You are not to reveal to anyone that Edora is an oracle nor are you to discuss it among yourselves lest someone overhear you."

With these last words the King sat, and General Morlay rose.

106

"All those in favor of tabling the decision of Havorth, say 'Aye'."

The council all shouted, "Aye!"

"All those…"

The door opened wide and a footman of the King appeared. The General looked over at the King with a raised eyebrow. King Beon nodded his reassurance and motioned for the footman to come to him. "One moment, my council. This may give us some clue or measure of certainty about the whereabouts of Edora."

The footman walked quickly toward the King, bowed, and handed him a note. The King nodded and said, "You may go. Thank you." And the footman retreated, face first, and removed himself from the room as the doormen closed the door quietly behind him.

After quickly perusing the note, the King rose again, as did the council in like kind. He motioned for them to resume their seats and said, "According to the gateman, a passage was given to a young maid last evening just before nightfall. It seems Edora has been resourceful and found a way to forge a letter in my handwriting granting her exit after dusk. But this means she left on foot just over a half-a-day ago. With resting time, she cannot have gotten far. I trusted she had taken to following the river north to Travessa and the gateman confirms that the log shows she exited and turned left, saying her mamá lived by the river. So, I believe we will be successful in our endeavors if we make haste in our decision."

The King sat and General Morlay, more confused than disgruntled about the turn of events, rose again and said, "All those in favor of sending out a scouting party for the attacker which will also operate as a search party for the white lady, say, 'Aye'."

"Aye!" the council all yelled back.

"Good, then, I want you three," and here the General pointed to the three closest to him on the right side, "to gather three scouts and be off within the half-hour. You may be able to find Edora by nightfall.

Follow the river. Send word back by noon of the morrow via one of you as to your discoveries. The rest of you continue on until you find Edora, the attacker, or both. If you find Edora, two of you bring her back immediately while the rest scout out the attacker and ride back with his whereabouts, his motives, the extent of his armament, and any information at all that might be helpful. Travessa is a two-day ride. Do not tarry more than five days. If we do not have you back in five days, we will assume you are lost and carry on without you. You have been ordered. Go now."

The three scouts rose, bowed to the King, saluted the General, and retreated to fulfill their duties.

The rest of the assembly was spent discussing procedures for arming the military and preparing them for another attack as well as general strategy for defensive postures if the attack came earlier than when they were fully ready. When the meeting ended, and the military council was excused from the room, General Morlay stayed behind for a word with the King.

"King Beon, why did you keep this oracle a secret even from me? As the General I should know about all matters of security and safety that pertain to you and to this kingdom. By not telling me, you put us in greater risk as the attack last week showed."

The General rarely spoke so freely to the King, but his incense at the King's distrust of him, and his embarrassment at being blindsided with this information at his own meeting, got the best of him.

"I do not regret it, Morlay, though I understand you are disposed to think otherwise. It was oracled to me by my Niamá to keep Edora hidden and safe. I do not believe that created the attack upon us. Edora's oracular gifts have many times staved off military disasters without your awareness, so, if anything, she has kept us much safer. However, this time, there is something else afoot that neither she nor I are completely aware of that puts not only us at risk, but this entire region. The man who has attacked us without honor has powers that we know not of. I reveal this to you alone. It is through these powers that he gained access to Havorth's mind and to the white lady's tower. We must prepare, not just militarily, but with cunning to match him. For this, we need the white lady."

"I still must protest. At any time during the last several days you could have informed me as to the nature of this attack and you did not."

"I, too, was unsure of the attacker's identity and his intentions until yesterday after the meeting hence. With Edora's escape, I am at even more loss as to the outcome of our next encounter with this man. And Morlay, I believe you to be an honest man with the best of intentions. However, if I had revealed to you the nature of Edora's gifts and the powers of the attacker would you have believed me? Do you believe me now?"

"I, uh," the General stammered, then regained his vocal footing. "You are my King. I will do as you command."

"That is what I believed of you, Morlay. You may go."

Morlay reddened at the King's slight back-handed compliment, then saluted, and made a hasty exit. In his retreat, the King, too, left, making his way back to his quarters to strategize what he would do if his scouts did not find Edora in time.

The scouting and search party left after gathering supplies for a five-day ride. The General saw them off. "Because Edora was on foot when she left, I believe you will be able to catch up to her by nightfall or by the latest, tomorrow morn. Rest and sleep as little as possible. You heard the King—time is of the essence. It appears more clouds are gathering. Did you prepare for the possibility of rain?"

"Yes," the party leader declared tersely.

"Good. I will expect one of you back with news by noon of the morrow, if not two of you with Edora. May speed be with you."

And with that they turned and galloped away toward the river and General Morlay returned to his troops for more drills.

As soon as the scouting party reached the river, they turned to the north and sped along its banks, through the charred remains of Shandar Forest, and off towards Travessa as fast as their slowest horse could keep the pace. After a couple hours of steady gains, they stopped for a short break and tracking. The grounds there were soft and mostly untraveled so the scouts, while off their horses, looked around for any trace of Edora or her footprints. If she had been on foot, they assessed they should be able to catch her soon. The hills ahead beckoned them on, but they and their horses needed the rest.

As the party let their horses graze, they searched around in the area just to the north of where they had stopped, where their horses had not stirred up their tracking endeavors. The scout who was farthest ahead, shouted, "Over here!"

The others ran to his side even as he motioned for them to stay behind his outstretched arms. Then he squatted, as did the others as he put his hand over the grassy turf.

"Look here. And here. What do you see?"

The scouts inched a little closer and eagle-eyed the ground.

"That looks like a hoofprint there," said one of the women as she pointed at the mark.

"Yes, but look again," said the first scout.

"It's shod," said another scout.

"Look even closer," the first scout admonished.

The scouts stepped forward again and were kneeling on the ground studying the prints.

"It's one of ours! I can see the lightening marking at the top of the shoeprint," a third scout exclaimed.

"Indeed," the first scout confirmed. "And these hoof and shoe prints up ahead all show the same markings. She's not on foot. She's astride a horse. I doubt we will catch up to her by nightfall or even tomorrow noon. It depends on how fast she's riding and how much she rested last night. If she even rested."

The search party leader then stood up. "Good work, scouts. But now we must ride faster as our task is harder. Get your horses to the river to drink and then we're off. We will not stop again till nightfall."

The scouts hurried to obey their orders, but luck was not with them, it seemed. Before they had even started off again, the rains had come, meaning tracking Edora would become next to impossible— the rain would erase all signs of prints.

By dusk, the scouting party had made it to the first village where Edora had been early that morning. The party leader asked around at several of the homes as to whether anyone had seen a young woman traveling through on horse or on foot. No one reported seeing anyone at all, other than fellow villagers. A shop owner who came to the door after hearing a knock had the same story but offered a clue. "No, I saw no one last night or since. However, the trough of hay in front of my shop was empty this morning when I went to open for trading. I always fill it full the evening before so it's ready for the morning and I know I did so last night. If you're wondering whether someone on horse has been through here, I'd venture to guess, yes."

"Thank you, sir. Your information has been very helpful. The King of Devor owes you a debt of gratitude. May we pay you for your time and for the hay with this gift?" The scouting party leader held out a gold coin with King Beon's image stamped on it.

"No, no, what am I going to do with that? Eat it? No, thank you for your thought and kindness but hay's replaceable and I have enough to eat."

"You are an honorable man. If ever you need the King's or our kingdom's assistance, please call on us."

"Thank you, thank you. If you need some place to rest tonight out of the rain you can use the barn behind the house."

"Your generosity speaks well of all your people. We will rest there and be gone at the first break of light next morn."

The scouts walked their wet selves and horses to the barn and hung their damp clothes on the stall doors and then dressed themselves in dry clothes. They whispered to each other that Edora must have traveled through the village last night or in the morning before the shop owners had opened and villagers appeared. That meant she could still be a half-a-day ahead of them. None of them felt much hope they would find her before they reached Travessa, as they fell into an uncomfortable sleep to the sound of rain hammering on the barn's tin roof.

Chapter Sixteen

As Edora and Saza followed along behind the old man who muttered to himself as he tottered forward, the mist turned to a sudden downpour. They traveled slowly and even after the rainfall increased, the man was not speeding up at all even though within a couple of minutes Edora was thoroughly drenched. *How far away from the village does he live?* Edora wondered to herself.

"Not far now, dear one," the old man called back, again it was as if he had heard her thoughts.

Edora sneezed and shivered. The turn in weather had taken its toll and she was feeling feverish and sick. *I can't go on too much longer like this,* she thought to herself.

"Not to worry, not to worry. I'll have you good as new in no time, dearie," the old man chuckled this time and hobbled along the trail into a small wooden grove, tucked away in the glen far up from the village.

No one will be able to see us up here or hear us, Edora thought with an alarm, and then realizing the old man was probably going to hear and answer her, she quickly added, *That will be good for hiding.*

"Yes, yes, good for hiding, indeed!" the old man chuckled again.

After making their way into the small wood, the trail narrowed, and they walked single file with Saza trailing behind her as she led him with the reins. Most of the downpour was not able to penetrate the canopy of leaves overhead, so at least she now had some respite from the chilled moisture.

The old man made a sudden turn and after following suit, she could see a little cottage up ahead. Smoke was billowing out of the chimney. A fire must already be going! Edora couldn't wait to warm up and eat food. She was unwilling to enter the cottage without knowing who he was, so she asked the old man, "Dear kind sir, may I have the pleasure of knowing whose house I am entering?"

"It's mine, silly!" the old man rasped back at her.

"Yes, but what is your name?"

"Uh-ho! She wants to know my name! But you should know that already."

"I'm sorry, sir, I wish that I did, but…"

The old man looked crestfallen that she still was totally perplexed by his presence. "Never mind. Never mind. Maybe that's the way it needs to be. Just call me Jaxper."

"Jaxper? What an unusual name. I am happy to meet your acquaintance, Jaxper. Thank you for your hospitality."

"Of course, my dearie, of course. And now let me take your horsey out to my barn to get some hay and shelter for the night. You go ahead in and rest up by the fire. I'll be in shortly to get you some of your own food. Hurry up, now, you're wet and cold. There you go." Jaxper held the door open to his cottage and then closed it behind him and led Saza off to the barn at the right.

Inside, the warmth coming from the fireplace beckoned her forward, though at first sight Edora was reminded again of her oracles of fire accompanied by screaming, and she hesitated. *What do they mean?* She concentrated hard but nothing came to mind. She didn't know if she would ever be comfortable looking straight at a fire, but her wet clothes and shivering body needed the dry heat. She sloshed her way to the hearth and stood before it, stretching out her hands, occasionally turning around to warm her backside as well. She kept her eyes tightly closed, in a futile effort to keep the troubling images at bay, as she basked in that hot air.

In a few minutes, Jaxper had entered the cottage and seemed pleased to see Edora warming herself. "Oh, good! You're already getting toasty. Your horsey is happy with hay and water and a good dry place to sleep tonight, and for you, I have a nice hot stew already made in the kitchen oven. I'll go and get it ready for us to dine, but stay by the fire for now, dearie," and off he wandered to a room behind the living area, a grin pasted to his wrinkly face.

Feeling slightly more hopeful with the thought, *Why would Jaxper feed me if he intended me harm?* Edora looked around at the cottage. *What an odd place,* Edora thought to herself. It was decorated with various wood totems of all sizes—some painted with garish oils and stains, some unpainted, some standing on the floor and some standing on tables of different heights—metal-worked windmills spinning from an unseen wind, iron cages with twittering, mechanical-like birds hung here and there, and earthenware bowls of water everywhere, being dripped in as if catching leaks from holes in the rain-drenched roof. But as far as Edora could tell, the drips were not coming from the interior roof and ceiling. Where they were coming from was a complete mystery to her, as she could see no source for the drips. Books were scattered everywhere, most open, others closed, and all with the same brown leather binding. *Maybe his trade is bookbinding,* contemplated Edora. In all, the cottage looked more like the art collection room or perhaps the history room that she'd seen many years ago in the King's castle when she'd first visited and toured, than like a residence for a human.

By the time Jaxper reemerged from the kitchen with the pot from the oven, Edora was feeling rather like she had just come out of the oven herself. The skin on the back of her hands was bright crimson and the skin on her face and the rest of her body felt just as flush. She walked over to the table Jaxper had carried the pot of stew to and tried to help clear space off the cluttered top to make room to sit down and eat. If it was supposed to be a dining table, it didn't appear to get much use as such.

"Oh, thank you, dearie. I'm not much for housekeeping as you can see." He chuckled and looked Edora right in the eye. She jumped back a bit, for when he looked at her this way, she had felt a spark in her own eye. Acting as if nothing had just happened between them, he continued, "If you can just take the books and put them all on the floor, I'll run back to the kitchen for some bowls and spoons."

Edora started picking up all the books on the table and stacking them into piles five high to the side of the table where no one could trip over them. The bookbinding was soft and supple with a moist grain. *Were they made of leather or wood?* Edora couldn't decide. She had never seen books such as these and she wanted to explore them further. Just as she was done with the stacking, Jaxper was back again with the bowls and spoons. He left once more "for some healing mead and mugs" and Edora placed a bowl and a spoon on either side of the table for her and the old man and sat down and waited for his return.

When Jaxper came back, there was something decidedly different about him. Edora wasn't sure. *Was he younger? His back straighter? His hair less gray?* Edora shrugged it off to her own fatigue. Jaxper sat down on the bench opposite Edora and scooped up heaping ladles full of stew for the both of them. Then he poured mead into both of their mugs and encouraged her, "Eat up and drink up for tomorrow we may die!"

Edora didn't like the sound of that at all and so she waited until the old man had eaten his first bite and drunk his first sip before she allowed herself to do the same. Her first bite of stew was delicious, especially after eating bread and cheese all day. She devoured the spicy venison chunks and root vegetables before sipping up the rest of the broth. The meal for both of them passed in silence with Jaxper taking an occasional glimpse at Edora that looked like he was assessing her every few bites. The tasty mead she saved mostly for last, as it was sweet and felt like liquid dessert to her mouth. Swirling it in her mouth she thought she could pick up a hint of sassafras or was it sarsaparilla? She was never very good with herbs and roots but wondered if Jaxper had made her a medicinal brew for her chills as she started to feel rummy all over.

"Indeed, I have, dearie. Indeed, I have," the old man broke the silence, again answering her silent thoughts with spoken words.

"Jaxper. How is it that you do that?" the mead had given Edora more courage to speak her mind. He apparently read her thoughts anyway—she might as well speak them out loud. "I think a thought in my own head, and then without a moment's delay you answer as if you've heard my innermost thoughts clear as a bell. How is that possible?"

"There are many things you don't know about me," Jaxper whispered across the table mysteriously.

"Like what?" Edora inquired.

"Like look around this room. How do the windmills blow when there is no wind? How do the drippings drop when there are no leaks? Hmmm?"

"I was wondering about those things too," and she pointed at the quirky totems.

"Oh, yes, the bridgestones. Yes, they're very magickal, indeed."

"Bridgestones? I thought they were totems."

"Oh, is that what you're calling them now?"

"What? I'm confused." Was it the mead that was confusing her brain or the old man? "I thought you were going to answer my questions not ask me questions."

"Not tonight, my dearie, not tonight. Tonight, you are going into a very deep sleep. Tomorrow morn we'll speak again."

And with that, Edora swooned and would have fallen off her bench, but lickety-split, the old man was around that table and behind her fast enough to catch her. *He sure is fast for such an old man*, thought Edora muddledly.

"Oh, yes, I am!" chuckled Jaxper through his words, as he helped Edora to a lounging chair tucked in the corner of the room.

The last sight she saw that night was the old man over her, tucking her in with a heavy woolen blanket, and as he looked in her eye one last time that night, again she felt the spark in her own eye, before drifting off to dreamless sleep.

The scouts and search party were up before dawn. Their leader tried to cheer his party up as they dressed for their ride, "The rains have stopped, and I can see the sky is clear." The scouts all knew, though, that they were still up to a half day behind Edora if she had ridden all day yesterday, and because the rains fell hard during the night, any type of foot or hoof prints would have been washed out in the deluge, thereby preventing any tracking of Edora at all. It had already rained after the attacker's departure and his rebels' well-set forest fire allowing their tracks to be erased as well, which is why the King hadn't established a search party for their attackers right away. Pointless. And back they were again to a pointless mission. It seemed something was set against them, something that did not want them to find Edora or their attacker.

Their leader sensed their minds and so rallied them. "We will press on to Travessa and be there before nightfall if we ride hard. That is the last known place of our attacker. I know there is a village between here and there and I suspect someone might have seen Edora or the band of men traveling through a few days ago, after our attack. One of us needs to ride back to Devor for this report. Any volunteers?"

No one stirred. "Good. I see you're all ready to complete your mission. Sayer. It is you who shall go and report. Make haste that you arrive in Devor by noon."

Sayer, the scout with the least experience, nodded in agreement. The rest of the party then ate a quick breakfast from their stores, drank from their pouches, and readied their horses. After leading them out of the barn, Sayer sped south toward Devor, while the other five rode to the north following the river. No one saw them leave.

That same morning, Edora awoke with a start. The few rays of sunlight that could make it through the dense tree canopy surrounding the cottage were streaming through the windows of the room she was in. *Where am I?* she wondered, looking around at the odd room. *Oh, that's right, I'm in the old man's home. What's his name again? Jaxper?* She slowly got up from the lounge chair she had slept in but didn't feel quite able to move around. Whatever he had given her to drink was still working its effects on her, making her feel very unsure of walking.

She stretched her hands up above and wiggled her toes. Though still a little woozy, her body felt better, like whatever ailment had tried to overcome it with chills and sneezes the night before had thought better of it and left. Jaxper was nowhere in sight. *Perhaps he's out in the barn attending to Saza.*

With a few deep breaths, Edora felt much more grounded and began roaming around the living area to explore the peculiar artifacts, trinkets, and books she had espied the night before. In the sunlight, nothing looked quite as mysterious or spooky as it had in the firelight, yet still there was something about them all that made her want to stay and become a student of Jaxper. It was as if the objects wanted her to touch them or open them or even play with them.

Edora was especially curious about the sourceless drips of water ceaselessly falling into the bowls. She approached a largish earthenware piece full to the brim with water and constantly being dripped in, yet it never overflowed or spilled. She bent over to look under the table it was resting on but could see no source or drain there either. Waving her hand through the air above where the drips materialized revealed nothing and waving her hand below where the drips appeared, she simply got her hand wet from the sole droplet of water that fell next. She smelled the water on the back of her hand but noticed nothing unusual and then risked licking the droplet—but not terribly surprising, it tasted like mere water. She pondered whether these bowls of water were scry-worthy yet not wanting to see any more flames or hear any more screams, she didn't try.

More perplexed than ever, Edora investigated the windlessly spinning windmills. She could detect no wind with her hand at any angle before or around the blades. It, too, was sourcelessly powered. When she got nearer to the birds, she saw they had all sorts of odd colors not found on birds in this region, though they acted typical of the birds she'd become fond of watching from her lonely tower in Devor. These almost looked painted. The books, too, mesmerized her and she found herself picking them up, feeling their soft hardness with her hands. To open them without permission felt like she would be breaking some law of privacy. They seemed to call to her, inviting her and giving her permission to open them.

One book in particular kept drawing her gaze to it and so she picked it up and held it between her hands. The urge to open it was strong, but she resisted and simply felt into the book. Pretty soon her hands were vibrating. She wanted to put the book down, but it was stuck to her hands. The hot vibration spread up her arms, along her shoulders, down her spine and within a few seconds her entire body was vibrating. Edora didn't know what was happening—only that the vibrating had reached such a strong intensity that her body was now pulsating in rhythmic lurches. She willed herself to stop but that did nothing.

How long can this go on? Where's Jaxper? Help!

And with relief, at that moment, Jaxper opened the front door to the cottage, saw Edora, and came to her rescue. Putting one of his hands on Edora's head and the other on the book, the pulsations stopped immediately, and she was able to take her hands off the book, while he took the book from her and placed it on a nearby table.

"What was that?" Edora queried him intensely.

"Oh, ho, good morning to you, too, dearie! I see you've met one of my friends. Books are your friends, you know. You must be careful with them, though. They're very, very tricky."

"But why was I vibrating and pulsating? What kind of book makes a person do that?"

"We're very inquisitive this morning, aren't we? 'What kind of book makes a person do that?' Why, a vibrating book, silly!"

"Yes, but…"

Jaxper held up his hand. "Enough questions for now, my dear. You've slept a long time. It's nearly lunch. Now's the time to eat and ask questions later. Follow me," and he turned around and waved her forward with his hand like he had done yesterday in the village square.

She followed him but could not resist engaging him with her thoughts—out loud as thinking them to herself was beside the point. "Why am I here? I really need to leave. I'm sure there are people looking for me and they could be at this village today. I must head out with Saza after lunch."

"I don't think so. You'll be here for another day. I have things to show you before you go."

"What sorts of things?" Edora wanted very much to know. They were now in what must be the kitchen though it was a makeshift one at best with pots and stools and utensils stacked and stored on every available surface. The fireplace in the living area backed up to this room with another cooking fireplace and oven all sharing a chimney.

"All sorts of things," Jaxper replied over his shoulder as he had gone to a cupboard and pulled out some bread and cheese. Wiping away dust off a countertop he placed the bread and cheese atop it and then gathered some plates sitting on a stool and handed them to Edora. "Take these and the bread and cheese, and I'll be out with some figs and drink in a jiffy."

Edora silently accepted her lot and did as was told. Asking Jaxper questions and getting any helpful answers was useless and she felt more exasperated than she'd ever felt in her life.
Befuddled, she set the table with the plates and food she was given and sat down to await Jaxper's return.

He bumbled in with mugs in one hand, a pitcher under his arm, and a bowl of dried figs in his other hand. "Ah, here we are. Well, dig in, what are you waiting for?" he quipped in his usual manner of expecting Edora to read his thoughts as easily as he read hers.

Edora ate reluctantly, pulling the bread in pieces, eating a fig here and there and generally unhappy with her state of affairs. Maybe she just needed to get up and leave. He was a small, old man and she was sure if it came to it, she could outrun him to the barn to hop on Saza and ride off after lunch. Yet, he'd said he had things to show her. Maybe she should stay and at least see what he had for her. He clearly had some type of magickal abilities. Maybe he could help her find the sorcerer.

For the first time, Jaxper did not respond to her thoughts.

Chapter Seventeen

The scouting party rode hard. Their leader knew the village that lay between them and Travessa was near, nestled in a hidden ravine in the hills. They hadn't stopped since they left at pre-dawn, and soon the horses would need water and rest. It was nearing noon and the scouts, too, needed food and a break.

They had seen no sign of Edora and never stopped to look for tracks since the rain had wiped out any hope of scouting her direction. If they didn't find her by the time they reached Travessa, their aim would be to search directly for their unknown attacker.

Just as they were nearing the village of Javenia, the scout who had ridden back arrived at Devor at the bidden time to update the King and the General with the scouting party's news.

Entering the castle's door, the scout made his way to the council chamber where he hoped both the King and the General were still present at the end of their daily strategy meeting with the rest of the military council.

The doorman knocked twice from the outside and awaited a "Here!" from the inside to signal that it was permissible to open the door. He then did so and allowed the scout to appear in the doorframe.

King Beon and General Morlay, upon seeing the scout, both motioned for him to enter. The doorman closed the door behind him, and the scout walked to the long table and waited for instruction. He was unaccustomed to council logistics, as he was not a member of these esteemed soldiers.

General Morlay looked at the scout and announced, "I assume since you are alone you did not find Edora as of this morning?"

"That is correct, sir."

"What other news do you have then?"

"Yesterday, we scouted the area north of the Shandar Forest, before the rains came, and found horse prints leading north. Horse prints shod with our military shoes. There were no footprints."

"Edora is on a horse?" the King asked alarmed.

"It appears so, sir. There were two or three unaccounted for after the fire attack. Perhaps she found one of them, my liege."

"I think that is safe to assume," the General said dryly. "So, how long till the scouts reach Travessa, assuming they don't find Edora today?"

"Plans were to reach Travessa by nightfall. We were deterred from riding last night due to the heavy rains, but they were able to start before dawn this morning and had no reason not to make it."

"Excellent. You may leave. Thank you, scout," the General nodded the report to an end and the scout turned and retreated face first.

After his departure, the General and King continued their deliberations with the council, assuming the worst now that Edora would not be found, at least not until they had also found their attacker.

While the returning scout delivered his report to King Beon and General Morlay, the rest of the scouting party arrived in Javenia. The market square was busy with many people trading their wares and root crops, conversing with neighbors, and tending to their livestock as children played hopping and hiding games with each other.

A few of the villagers turned to gawk at the five military scouts who rode in on horses—most ignored them. The scouting leader dismounted, and the rest followed suit as he walked to a farmer's booth, "Kind sir, we are traveling through here in search of a woman. We have some questions to ask but first we must attend to our horses' needs. Is there a place they can graze freely or a store with hay and oats to purchase for their food?"

"Ah, yes, sir, behind my booth I have some feed. What are you offering me for trade?"

"I have the King of Devor's coins. They are good in our great kingdom-city for purchasing any needs you might have."

"Devor, you say? That's a day and a half's ride if you're riding hard, two or three if you're not in a hurry. What could I purchase with your King's change?"

"There are many fine artisans and metalworkers who make valuable pieces that could only benefit your farming, beyond what your fine villagers provide here."

"There is, is there? Well, alright, then. I'll take you up on it. Give me five coins per bale and bucket of oats?"

"Agreed. Thank you for your generous trade with our kingdom. Please consider yourself a friend."

"Thank you. Thank you. And you said you had some questions?"

"Yes, let me get our team started feeding and watering our steeds and I'll be back soon."

"Sure enough," the farmer nodded, stroking his beard with his right hand and jingling his newly acquired coins in his left. He watched the scouting party lead their horses to the grazing area behind his booth, then pulled out a bag that hung around his neck beneath his shirt. After stuffing his newly acquired coins in it, he hid it under his shirt again, and went back to ordering his booth.

When the scout leader had secured his steeds with food, he left his scouts with the horses and returned to the farmer.

"We are looking for one of our own, a woman on a horse. She probably traveled through here sometime late yesterday. She is in danger from our attackers who set fire to our forest last week."

"Oh yes, we could see the smoke from that fire from here," the farmer mused with eyes that widened upon hearing the word fire.

"But did you see her, or did you happen to see a band of men last week ride through here?"

"We try not to pay too much attention. Keeps us out of harm's way, you know? There were a lot of men traveling through here about a week ago. Didn't stop. Didn't talk. I don't know where they came from or where they were going. The woman—I haven't seen."

"Do you think it will be okay if I ask around the village?"

"Oh sure, it's fine. I just wouldn't be expecting too much, though. People keep to themselves here."

"Thank you. You have been most helpful."

The scout leader made his rounds around the market square asking about Edora with traders and villagers alike. No one could say they had seen her. No one could say much of anything, though they remembered the band of men riding through the town many days before.

After seeing that any more questions would simply be spinning wheels, the scout leader returned to his team and their horses behind the market square. They were chatting quietly among themselves as they ate from their stores and the horses nibbled fresh hay and oats.

"I've been able to ascertain that a large group of men rode through this village about a week ago. Who they were, what they were doing, and where they were going, I could not find out, as they rode through without stopping or talking. Based on the timing of the villagers' observations, I would say that the men were our attackers. The odd thing is that no one noticed Edora ride through here. So, either she again made her way during the night or she has gone in a different direction than what we can know or track at this time."

"Are we riding straight on to Travessa then?" asked another scout.

"Yes, that is our aim—to scout Travessa and the surrounding area to see if we can ascertain the whereabouts of our attackers and who they are, and then return to Devor with any information that may help us defend our fair kingdom-city.

"Be ready to ride in a few minutes. I hope to be at Travessa before dusk so we can begin scouting and inquiring tonight."

After finishing their lunch and attending to the last of their horses' needs, the scouting team was off. No one from the village noticed their leaving.

The meal ended without any conversation. Each kept their heads bowed over their food until the last morsel was consumed. As she began to gather up her dishes, and Jaxper his, the silence grew too much for Edora's nerves. She placed the dishes back on the table with a bit too much of a thud. "Sir…Jaxper, I am too pent up to stay without knowing what I am here for. Since you first saw me, you have seemed to know all about me, even my every thought. I am at a disadvantage. I know not who you are, nor why I am here. I have a mission I am on and I must attend to this. Any delay will only bring more doom to people I love. I cannot stay unless you are forthcoming as to my purpose here."

Jaxper sighed and put his dishes back on the table as well. "Why don't we sit in the front room. There is something you ought to know. I'm surprised you don't remember but it is clear I am going to have to tell you." Jaxper walked to a chair and sat and motioned for Edora to follow. She hesitated. *Did she really not remember? That was not like her. She had a good memory. Who was Jaxper and why did he know her?*

Edora was about to find out. She would regret her memory lapse of the man transforming in front of her.

Chapter Eighteen

The scouts flew, riding on the backs of their steads into the biting wind. It nipped at their skin like an attacking dog as the winter sun stared coldly at their backs. If all they knew of life came from these moments, they would only know that the world was an unfriendly, even hostile place to live.

Travessa came into view, rising above the plains like an emerging flood. The scout leader understood from long experience judging distances from afar that they would reach their destination before dusk. They had seen no sign of Edora, no sign of anyone or anything. It was barren and desolate this side of Javenia. The plains would not be fertile again until the other side of Travessa where the river Cressic ran fast. Within an hour as the sun was falling from its shallow perch like it too was tired and spent of riding the skies for so long unhindered, the scouting team drove to the gates of the great kingdom-city Travessa.

They made it well before dusk and therefore had opportunity to inquire of the city's guards.

The lead scout approached the right-standing guard of the city's main gate. "We are servants of the King of Devor, sent on a mission to scout our attackers who set fire on our city without warning and without honor. We have heard there were a band of men, of roughriders, near Travessa who may be the ones we seek. Do you have any news of such men?"

The city guard set his chin and stamped his spear in standard reply. "We have no such men in Travessa. We have seen no such men through these gates in many moons. However, if you travel west along the river Cressic there was a band of men who made camp there. They have given us no trouble, and we have given none to them. If you find and have any interaction with them, you will not mention this report or Travessa."

"Agreed. Whatever I discover I will report back to you if you wish."

"Agreed."

"Is there a place near this gate we can feed and water our horses before we scout this camp? They are weary from a day of riding hard."

"If you follow the road of the city around to the north you will discover a trading post that will welcome your gifts in exchange for supplies for your scouts and your steed."

"Thank you. We consider you friends of Devor and her King. Please seek us if you are ever in need. Give thanks to your Queen."

The sentry guard nodded and stamped his spear, giving indication that the conversation was over.

The scouting party dismounted and walked their horses to the outpost fearing the worst for Edora but hopeful they would soon have information about their attackers to bring back to their King.

King Beon and General Morlay had spent days rehearsing different strategies for fortifying their walls and security. With the natural barrier of the Shandar Forest gone, they had redoubled the training efforts and the numbers of their soldiers and set their outlook posts far beyond the outside boundaries of the charred remains of the forest. They could see no way a band of men on horses could do them any harm now. So how would the attack come? The King knew he was dealing with a man whose power he could not fathom, let alone defeat. How could his army prepare for cunning and evil he could not foresee? And with Edora gone and perhaps even in the hands of this unknown sorcerer, Devor's fate was even less perceivable. The King dreaded the news to come from his scouts. What would he do without Edora if death befell her? His fears betrayed how much he had come to depend on her. She steadied him, grounded him, and at the same time, painted astonishing colors in his black and white, duty-bound world. He was drawn to her in ways he couldn't articulate even to himself. But he was weary of his fears, and his mind tried to wrest control away from the worst forecasts of doom that followed him in his dreams and his every straying thought.

The day had been filled with training drills and poring over maps, drawing diagrams of various tactical formations on them. The King was seated in the Great Room with the General and senior officers for a hasty lunch—all he allowed time for these days. One of the immense wooden doors of the room opened and the doorman bowed as the scout entered. The King looked intently at his soldier's face to read whatever might be written on the lines there. Nothing. He could see the scout had little-to-no news.

"My liege," the scout saluted.

"Yes," General Morlay said, his voice taut. "You have returned home in the expected time. Well done. What news have you?"

"We have news but not good news, I am afraid. First, Edora was never seen and we lost her tracks after the rainfall. Her whereabouts remain unknown."

Morlay responded tersely, "Yes, the first scout back reported such."

The scout cleared his throat nervously and continued, "Second, we made our way to Travessa and were informed that there had been a camp of men outside their borders near the Cressic river. We found the area of their encampment, but it was deserted. It appeared that they left in a hurry and perhaps continued west following the river, but it was impossible to tell, as the rains also washed out their tracks. We know that they likely were gone before we had even left to scout them. We tried to pick up their tracks again but were without success before we had to turn back to return to you by noon today."

Here he moved forward toward a map that was laid out on the table in front of the officers and pointed to the spot on the river that was where they were forced to turn around for time constraints and continued, "That is all that we were able to procure. The guard at Travessa gave us the information about the camp but was quick to

130

dissociate the city from these men and wanted no interference from them or us. We sent word, per our agreement, that the men had disembarked from camp. Then we rode here to give our report. I regret we were unsuccessful at recovering Edora or finding the men who attacked Devor."

"Did the villages you stopped at on the way have any word?" the General continued his line of questioning with the scout.

"The farther village of Javenia reported widely that they had seen a band of men traveling through about a week ago but had not seen Edora. They had no further information as the men rode through the villages without stopping or speaking but based on the time schedule and the description, I am sure they were our attackers. The first village, Frentia, had no specific information about anyone except that hay in a feeding trough had recently gone missing. Perhaps, this indicates that Edora had been there, but we have no way of knowing, sir."

"So, did it appear the men returned to their camp on Cressic before they decamped?" the King asked, squinting his eyes at the map for any insight it might reveal. He looked much like Edora when she scried the waters, searching for the visual clues they imparted.

"It would appear so. The firepit ashes were more of a few days old, rather than two weeks old. Still they were a week ahead of us," the scout relayed.

"Yes, yes, of course, you did not have the time to pursue them. That is no fault of you or your team. We commend you for your excellent service. Thank you. You may go. If we have any further questions, we will call for you. In the meantime, rest today and tomorrow rejoin the troops for training exercises," Morlay was restless. The information his scouts provided was next to useless. No more talk. It was just spinning time.

"My lord," the scout bowed and retreated face-first, striding backward across the echoing hall's floor in deliberate measure.

After the doorman closed the door and retreated, General Morlay addressed the King. "Sir, we are with no more information than five days ago. What a waste!"

"Not necessarily, General. We have procured the probable trajectory of their departure to be the westward flow of the river Cressic. That may give us some insight. If they mean to attack us, perhaps it will be from the southerly route of the Bedoga river that crosses the Cressic here farther west than the encampment our scouts found." King Beon pointed to the point on the map. The other military council members inched closer in their chairs to have a better look at the map on the table.

The King continued, "I will give leave to you right now. Keep up the drills. Let us commence our deliberations in two hours hence."

And with that the King rose, followed by the rise of everyone at the table as they stood while the King exited into his private quarters.

Dayud drove his men harder. Beyond the edge of sanity, his fury fueled the intensity of his revenge. There was more work that had to be done to harness the energy of the water to his ends. The first time, he had attacked with fire. This time he would have his vengeance with the element that had eluded his control: water. As his men toiled, he retreated to his tent. Something was drawing his attention, but he could not bring it to focus. Perhaps a silent moment would catalyze the formation of the awareness. He stood in the tent and brought his thoughts into his fiery soul. There emerged an image. The woman he had sought was coming to him, walking toward him. She would be there soon. But how? How could she find her way to him? No matter. He would soon have the revenge he sought against her and then he would unleash his rage on the city that had shielded her from him. He returned to the work of his men, but his mind was occupied, plotting the use of Edora against Devor.

Many hours later, Edora was still trembling. Jaxper had revealed himself and his powers. She had never had to use her own powers to such an extent as she had earlier in the day, but she had accomplished what needed to be done and was on her way past Travessa with her faithful Saza. She knew now what her mission was and what she had to do. Whether she was successful in stopping the coming hell or not, the road towards the sorcerer was her destiny and nothing would persuade her otherwise.

Using her divining tools, she had mapped out the sorcerer's location. Her tools had pointed her away from Travessa, much farther away than she would have guessed without her unique skills. The tools had also shown her that the sorcerer was at the intersection of two rivers. In Travessa she had made a quick stop to ascertain from some tradesman selling tools, where the intersection of two rivers to the southwest of the Travessa might lay. She was told there was only one such landmark for many miles all around.

It was there that she was headed now though the darkness had settled into the day and the night was thickening. She hoped to be at the sorcerer's camp by the morning, no later than noon. The element of surprise would help her, but with his own gifts, she could not count on the sorcerer being unaware she was on her way to him. She only hoped she could stop the doom that continued to reveal itself in her mind's eye.

The King retired to his bedchamber for a rare retreat. As he entered, his servants, surprised to see him at this hour in midday, exited quickly and quietly. He sat on the edge of his bed, head in his hands. Edora was gone, perhaps never to return. He could not imagine life without her. He had lived for many years without an oracle before she had appeared, but now he knew she meant more to him than as simply his oracle. What would he do to get her back? What could he do? What was he willing to do? His first duty was to his Devor, but how could he protect both? He had no idea. Nothing came to mind. His only hope was that Edora's gifts could protect her. He sat for a few more minutes following the lines of worry furrowed on his brow with his fingers as if reading the lines of fortune on a hand: carefully, methodically, intentionally. Like walking a labyrinth, it calmed him and centered him. Suddenly, an image rushed into his mind's eye like water when a dam's gates opened suddenly. He knew his next move.

Retracing his steps back the way he came, he entered through the large wooden door that connected his private residence to the Great Room where his General and military advisors would soon reconvene. He was glad that this time, he had a strategy to offer.

As the new day dawned, Edora crested a small hill, she saw trees in the near distance. They likely lined a river in this dry terrain, the river the sorcerer's camp would be next to, if her divining was accurate. She would arrive within an hour. Not wanting Saza to suffer her fate if she failed, she had offered him to a band of travelers a few miles back on an old trade route. Saza whinnied when she hugged him good-bye. She couldn't bear to look at him again and so forged ahead. Making her way on foot with measured slowness, her feet got heavier, her will less certain with each step. She had to stop.

Her heart pounded with trepidation, but she sat nonetheless and drew her mind deep into her soul. What appeared to her there was a plant, well the hint of a plant—a delicate green seedling in a barren landscape, alone and fragile. It resonated with her feelings about herself her entire life—at least until she had been the King's oracle for the past several years. In Devor, she had grown and learned her strength. The young plant grew in her mind into a large towering tree, its roots reaching deeply into the layers of time. As she meditated on this image her energy within her stirred. She was connecting with something she had learned in Jaxper's presence. She called on this now. She saw how her near future unfolded. She saw what she would be required to do. The sorcerer could defeat her. She knew it. She also knew she had within her a force that he could never touch, that he could never destroy. Her fear evaporated. She would willingly give her physical life if it would save so many.

134

She opened her eyes and saw two men riding to her on their horses. Edora intuited they were the sorcerer's men.

It had begun.

As the men approached Edora, she clutched her tools hidden under her embroidered dress for safe keeping. She would keep them close to her, hoping they might come in use without being discovered. As her right hand lay over them, she said a blessing, then dropped her hand and walked on ahead, praying, whispering that the spirits might protect her from the worst that she had seen.

The men rode up and stared with glaring eyes. *Menacing* was the word that came to Edora's mind.

The horserider on the right spoke: "We have come to bring you to our Master. He knows who you are and why you are here. You will come or we will force you. We do not think he will show you mercy."

"I am here of my own free will and will go with you without force. What will happen is not entirely up to him."

The second rider laughed under his breath. "She will learn," he sneered.

"How are you suggesting we arrive together? I am on foot. Will one of you carry me behind you or do I walk the rest of the way with the two of you as an escort?" Edora queried.

"You will ride with him," the first rider announced. The second rider's sneer immediately left his face but without delay, he walked his horse beside Edora, and took his foot out of the stirrup so she could use it, and with the help of his arm reached out holding on alongside hers she was able to leverage her weight enough to swing around behind him.

"Don't think of attempting anything against me. You will not win," her rider warned.

"You forget, sir. I have come to meet your Master of my own volition. Why would I try to harm you? To get away?"

Silence was the only reply she got—silence along with the snap of reins and the jerk forward of the gray Arabian, and it was only in silence they galloped the rest of the way to the camp.

Edora dismounted the Arabian first and stood while her escort and rider did as well. Then the first rider ordered him, "Stay here with her. I will return with our Master."

The second rider nodded while glaring at Edora. Edora ignored his poisonous eyes and breathed deeply into her center, praying. Praying to her spirits and the spirits of Devor: *Help me, I pray. Help me with what I must now do. I know the trials that are before me. I may not succeed. I may not even live, but let me be the salvation of my adopted people. Help me to save Devor. Help me to…*

She stopped suddenly as she felt a searing pain through her abdomen. *What?* And with her question she opened her eyes and saw the sorcerer coming toward her with an intense gaze directed at her midsection. She remembered him. Dayud. The look in his eyes. Somehow in her visions of him, his eyes were changed, hidden. She had not recognized him. But something about his razor-sharp stare jolted her memory. She did know him. A long time ago. What she didn't know, she was about to learn.

"So, you come of your own accord to challenge me? To stop me? You will not be successful, but I am so glad you are here, so I do not have to go and track you down again. You escaped me once but for what? Only to walk to my camp?"

"I am only here to offer myself. Take me, spare Devor."

"Oh, behold, a martyr." Dayud and his two men laughed. "You think that by giving me what I want I will save your fair but fire-burned city any more travail? What a fool!" Dayud mocked.

"I can only offer what I have."

"Then I will use you to break them for hiding you from me! Seize her!"

The rider beside her grabbed her wrists first and tied them in front of her with a rope from his horse's saddle. She gave no resistance. Now was not her test. She was led forward by the tug of the rope into Dayud's tent. Once he saw she gave no resistance and spoke nothing, he left her there and he went to command his men. "Now that we have the oracle, I will use my powers to bring Devor to its knees as revenge for shielding her from me. I will rebuild and enlarge its lands and become the great sorcerer of fire. Finish your work and stand guard. I will leave with this seer to the mountain of fire to break her and return in three days' time. Then I will finish what was started many years ago."

The King was back in the Great Room of Devor giving orders, outlining instructions, and planning his attack. He could only hope the sudden insight he'd had, had come from the beyond, maybe an oracle from the spirit of his Niamá. It was all he had to go on, but it made sense and the direction it gave him seized him with a ferocity he had never known. After another hour of conversation with his General, he was ready.

"Prepare the horses. We leave in an hour. Do not waste any time. Surprise may be impossible with a sorcerer, but he is arrogant and brash and may not even think to foresee that we are onto him. General, give your next-in-command the instruction and duty list for protecting Devor while we are away. Impress upon him the absolute necessity of reaching every citizen of Devor by tonight. If they tarry, they may perish. It is that essential."

"Of course, my King." The King's action inspired him. His will was resolute. *That's how a king should lead*, he thought to himself. The General was pleased and truly impressed for the first time with his monarch. He bowed, turned, and left.

In an hour the King with five dozen of his best soldiers, along with his General, set out north by the river Bedoga.

They would follow the road along the river up until it neared Frentia and then would ride directly north. Though wilder and rougher, the route away from the river held advantages. No one would see them approaching either village on the way toward Travessa, lest scouts of their enemy might be warned by their approach. It would get them to their target faster. However, it was also more dangerous. Steep ravines and narrow trails cut through mountains were treacherous for them and their horses. And there were many unknowns beyond the potential impact of the wilder terrain that could doom them to failure: unexpected turns in the weather and limited supplies not lasting if something occurred that they had not anticipated. Still the troop hoped to arrive right after sundown of the next day, a day and a half after they'd begun, to have the cover of darkness to hide their approach.

After about an hour ride, Dayud and Edora reached the mountain of fire, the site where Dayud had mastered the element of fire under the tutelage of his now deceased Master. Dayud dismounted first and then pulled a bound Edora off the back of his horse and led her to a cave he had frequented many times.

A surprise visitor was on his way.

Chapter Nineteen

The General was setting the pace hard for the first day. They had the good fortune of clear skies and calm winds to help their travel. They stopped at the end of the day at the foot of a mountain. They ate from their rations carefully, some bread and some cheese. They knew they might be in battle the next night and then what would come might seriously deplete the limited amount they were able to store on their horses for a fast ride. They let the horses scrounge for dry grass and fed them vegetables and fruit, then led them to water from a nearby pond.

General Morlay noticed the King pacing beside the pond. He was not sure why the King was certain they were on the right track, following a lead that only the King knew about. Of course, the King had admitted to him that he used oracles, but the King's only oracle was either captured or missing after running away. How could the King know that their enemies were vulnerable for only two days and at a certain location? Did the King use other magick, other sorcery to know the future that he didn't want to disclose?

Morlay shuddered at the thought of such unnatural things. In his view, these powers were best left alone, if they were even real. Mostly, he thought of these powers as fairy tales and rumors based on children's ghost stories. He didn't really believe in them. He would never consult an oracle himself and it appalled him that the King used oracles to protect the kingdom. Nevertheless, Devor had existed peacefully for many years, avoiding many conflicts. Even with the fire attack, the King had somehow known about it beforehand. If he as the General had relied simply on his scouts' reports, they would have been ambushed and perhaps destroyed. He couldn't argue with the remarkable accomplishments of his King. He decided to put his thoughts on the King's irregularities aside and simply follow his duty. If this was the King's secret to his great rule, then who was he to question it? He didn't know if it was real. He didn't know if it was wise. But he would not let it get in the way of information that could help them defeat a dishonorable enemy. He would ponder the questions at a later date, when leisure was the only duty of the day.

Edora was quiet throughout the ride to the mountain. At least she hadn't been blindfolded so she could see the exact route they had taken. Now that she was at the foot of the mountain, knowing what her task would be, she was prepared. Resolute.

She watched as the sorcerer tied up his horse to a well-worn post. This was a familiar place for him. She could sense his ease and even his routine pattern in how he walked toward the post and hitched the rein to it. *He feels almost at home here*, Edora thought to herself. She closed her eyes and let the images that were always flowing through the background of her mind to come to the fore and show her what she needed to know.

Several images appeared all jumbled: A river diverted, the King riding hard on his horse, a fire exploding uncontrollably, a death— no, many deaths. She breathed deeply, trying to make sense of the kaleidescoping images. How did they connect? What was the thread that tied them all together? She was here for a reason. Would she prevail or would she fail her beloved Devor?

"Come here, now!"

The sorcerer's demand startled her to full awareness. She blinked away the images from her mind's eye, pushing them into the background once again.

Edora stayed put. "May I please know the honor of your name?"

"Absolutely not. You know full well the power of knowing a sorcerer's name. You may call me Master, for your Master I am. I know your name well, though, Edora."

Edora kept her eyes focused not on Dayud but just behind him. She refused to let their souls see each other—yet.

140

"Are you surprised I know your name? I am more powerful than you, more powerful than anyone who has ever lived in our times. I will use you to become even more powerful, owning all of the lands as far as the eye can see, as far as the horses can run."

Edora again kept her eyes averted and didn't answer Dayud. She knew who he was. She even knew his name. What she didn't know, was how he had arrived at such a dark place in his heart with so much hatred and so much hunger for power.

His face distorted and he looked at her in disgust, at her refusal to bow to him, to call him Master.

"We move now, into the heart of the mountain, where I will break you. Then you will call me, Master."

Dayud grabbed Edora's left elbow, pinching it hard, forcing her to move forward with him. She didn't resist, but she was not eager for what was about to ensue.

The passage into the mountain was narrow and dark. Edora's elbow throbbed where Dayud held her, but she was grateful he knew his way around. How did he? It was too dark for human eyes. Was it memory? Did he have second sight? She could not deny a powerful sorcerer might have alternative manners of vision. But he seemed to know it more from familiarity she guessed, like her knowing the way her mamá walked when deep in contemplation, or how her papá stood smiling in the doorway when he came home from his day's work as a carpenter in the village square—with ease.

Dayud said nothing to her until they were through the passageway and had entered into a cavernous opening. Edora could see now. Torches lit the domed room, placed at even intervals around the perimeter. It was partially manmade, she observed: the rockface of the dark walls was hewn in places with blades to create a perfectly half-round space. In the center of it all was a massive fire. The smoke and heat suffocated her. There was only one small outlet at the very top of the cave—a chimney hole crudely carved into the rock. Edora felt like she was about to pass out from the lack of oxygen.

I can't breathe, she thought to herself. *How will I be able to do this if I can't breathe?*

Gentle words, reassuring words, formed in her mind. *Don't grasp for the air. Let it come to you. I am here with you.*

Jaxper! That's Jaxper's voice! Edora thought to herself. He had somehow established a telepathic connection to her. So much excitement bubbled up in her, she nearly forgot to heed his advice. After a gagging cough from too much smoke, she let her breath go in and out more gently and was relieved to feel the air come easier. The panic that had arisen her had not helped her body or her mind. She had to monitor her fear if she wanted to get out of this alive.

"I demand that you use the fire to see what your King does. Tell me or you will die," Dayud demanded with derision in his darkened eyes.

"I don't know what you mean, 'use the fire'," Edora answered honestly.

"You are a seer like your Mother before you. Use the fire to see the future."

"I don't use fire to see. I use water."

"Then I will make you bow to fire until it masters you and you will see from fire as I demand you."

Fire erupted from his palm. He held it as a ball, even passing it back and forth between his hands, then throwing it at a stick lying on the cave floor near the bonfire, where it erupted into burning wood.

"Look. Look into the fire. What do you see?"

"I see nothing but flame and destruction."

"Liar! You see more. You fail to speak truth."

Dayud again created fire in his palm. He held it close to Edora's face. She could feel the heat searing her skin, breathing threat into her pores. She refused to flinch. She looked down and inward, trying to transmit thoughts back to Jaxper. She had no idea whether she was successful or not. She could only hope he was helping from afar.

In a moment, the flame was extinguished. Dayud gasped.

"What did you do? How did you master it?" he demanded.

"I did nothing except focus within," Edora answered as matter-of-factly as she could, even though she could feel her limbs trembling, could sense her base instincts urging her to flee.

"Not possible!" he screamed. And again, there was a flame dancing on Dayud's palm, even larger than the last one and he held it even closer to Edora's face.

Again, Edora felt the tongues of fire licking her. She closed her eyes and looked inward. She saw the swirling of water, the tidal pool's circumference growing—the flow of water extending outward drawing nearer and nearer the edge of a waterfall. Edora's mind flowed with the spread of the water and then within her mind the water fell in an giant splash of cascading spray.

"No! You have extinguished the flame again!" Dayud's eyes betrayed his fear, darting back and forth from his palms to Edora's face.

Edora watched as Dayud reached towards her, hands empty of flames.

He grabbed her shoulders pulling her close to the bonfire. Flames flickered at Edora's cloak. The intensity of the heat overpowered her awareness. She started to feel herself grow faint, about to lose consciousness. "Stay awake!" She heard Jaxper's voice again, snapping her back to alertness. She felt like she was under some type of drug. Was Dayud burning a sleeping herb? A hallucinogen? Some magick that cast a spell with fire?

Edora closed her eyes. She felt herself begin to drift into some altered state of awareness. Dayud spoke forcefully but hypnotically. Somewhere in the background Edora heard another voice that seemed familiar. She couldn't quite place it. Was it another man? Yes. But who? Her head spun like a whirlpool. Then her whole body lurched, and she was lifted high above the fire. She looked down at the scene below. Why was she up here? She could see her body lying on the floor next to the fire. Dayud was saying what sounded like incantations in some unknown language.

Edora looked around and saw a transparent Jaxper floating near her. "Jaxper! What are you doing here? I thought you were still at your home in the woods!"

Jaxper chuckled. "I am. And I am here with you."

"How is that possible?"

"Never you mind. I'm here to help. You're out of your body and so at least Dayud's incantations will have no more effect on you here."

"What do you mean I'm out of my body?" Edora's confusion triggered panic rising in her chest or her so-called chest. When she looked down at herself, she saw she, too, was transparent.

"Well, you see your body down there, correct? And yet, here you are up here looking down on it all, from a vantage point that is far away from your body."

"Does that mean I've died?"

"No, no, not that." He chuckled again. "It could mean that, but no you are very much alive. I was concerned about the hypnotic effect Dayud was having on your mind, so I assisted in lifting you out of your body for safe keeping. Your body is simply sleeping now."

"When will I go back? Can I go back?" she felt panic rise in her etheric chest again.

"Yes, you can go back—anytime, but let's wait until the time is right. Dayud is still very dangerous, though not as dangerous as he likes to think he is."

Edora watched as Dayud's incantations grew louder and more manic. She wasn't sure what he was trying to accomplish, but she felt eerie all the same.

"What are we waiting for, Jaxper?"

"Dayud is weakening himself. He is trying to weaken you, but you are currently unaffected being that you're up here with me. He is unaware of your soul's departure. We need to let him use up as much of his power as possible, before you return to your body and do your own magick."

Edora knew to what Jaxper referred. He had coached her on what to do with her skills in order to hopefully defeat Dayud and save Devor. She had not known exactly what the circumstances would be—she really did not expect she would be out of her body waiting for the right time. She looked at Jaxper and thought, "Thank you" and he smiled and nodded, having received her telepathic thought instantly.

"Oh! This should be interesting," Jaxper looked up suddenly and floated higher out the room's chimney hole and was hovering just above it looking away into the far distance. He signaled for Edora to come up, too.

She didn't know how to do that exactly, but then she had the thought to go up and in the next instant she was beside Jaxper.

She looked off to where Jaxper's gaze was focused and saw a distant figure riding in on a horse. "Do you know who he is?"

"No, but I think you might," Jaxper answered.

"Really? I don't recognize him."

"I believe he was from your past, a long time ago. You may not recognize him. You were a child, he's a bit older."

Edora stared at the approaching figure. As she looked, his face zoomed in and she could see his features. She recognized him, but not from the past. He was one of Dayud's men who had accompanied her when she surrendered to Dayud. How could he be from her past? She shook her head, trying to remember anything having to do with him.

"I don't recognize him at all," Edora repeated, "I really don't. Who is he?"

Jaxper answered, "I don't know. But the thing is, my dear, he recognized you. What he is planning, though? I am not quite sure. We'll have to watch from this safe distance."

The man rode quickly toward the mountain, head down over his galloping steed, dark cape floating out behind him.

Edora felt herself drift down toward her body.

"No dearie! There'll be none of that!" Jaxper zapped her energy with a buzzing sound in her ears and drew her back up toward him, laughing under his breath, as he often did.

"What just happened, Jaxper?"

"I was distracted by the approaching rider and lost my focus for a second and Dayud started to draw you back with his magick. Won't happen again." He chuckled.

"He's almost here!" Edora pointed at the rider who had now dismounted and tied his horse to the same stake Dayud's horse was tied to. He patted down the horse briefly and gathered a stick with cloth around it, broke a flint on a stone to start a fire and within a few moments, his torch was aflame. He placed the torch in front of him, breathed deeply, almost seeming to draw power from the fire, and entered the mountain cave.

Jaxper nodded to Edora and they descended back through the chimney-like hole at the top of the cave, where they hovered above the scene of Dayud's incantations over Edora's body.

"This is so strange," Edora thought to herself and knew Jaxper had heard, for yet again, he chuckled.

Suddenly, Dayud's head snapped up from its focus on Edora's body. He looked in the direction of the cave entrance.

"How dare you intrude! How dare you interrupt me! Begone or you will face the full fury of my wrath!" Dayud yelled at his rider.

The cloaked man stepped into the cave and Edora and Jaxper could now see him, torch held high.

"Master. Forgive my intrusion. I have information that might be of use to you and your mastering of this woman."

"I don't need you to tell me anything. I can see everything that I must accomplish. Your presence is a distraction only. Leave. NOW!"

"Master, I know this woman. Or I did," the rider confessed.

"You are in grave danger by not obeying my orders immediately. Tread carefully, Makum."

"This woman, I remember her from my childhood. I knew as soon as I saw her. She stands out the same in her looks as she did then, white skin and white blonde hair. Not easy to forget as the fair do not live among us. She stood in the road after selling wares with her mother, at the time, a girl. I wanted her for myself, but she refused me. She defied me and denied me my right to take her," he was yelling at his Master, unafraid and aggressive.

Edora gasped, knowing now who he was. The memory flashed before her. She would never have recognized him, except from his anger. He was much changed from that older boy that had so arrogantly spoken to her. That she remembered vividly.

"If you knew her, why did you not speak of it to me whence she came to us," Dayud demanded.

"I hid it from you, because I wanted her for myself. I still do, Dayud. She was mine. I claimed her then. I did not know she still lived. I set the barn on fire where she and her mother lived and believed I had claimed her life then. Since my claim was made many years ago, it still stands. I claim her for myself now. You cannot have her. She is mine." Makum stood defiant.

Edora hung above the scene. If she had been in her body, she would've fainted at this revelation. This man, Makum—she had not even known his name—had been the one to set the barn aflame— the consequences of which had eventually taken her Mother, her dear mamá. She felt grief rise within her and Jaxper whispered telepathically, "My dear Edora. Your mamá is fine. Stay focused. You may grieve again in time. Stay focused. There is still danger here."

Edora imitated sucking in her breath. Since she was out of body, there was no breath, but her physical mannerisms remained. Focusing again on the unfolding scene, she put thoughts of her beloved mamá out of her mind but with a growing sense of doom.

"How dare you defy me! I made you, Makum! You learned your fire magick from me. I own you. And I own Edora. You have no rights here. Leave now and maybe I will forget your insolence and betrayal."

Makum took one step closer and breathed in the flickering fire from his torch, then blew it in a targeted blast toward Dayud.

It never reached him. The flame stopped mid-air, frozen in place as if in a painting. Dayud chanted, "Nevo devum" over and over in a low growl, pointing at the flame, it moved toward Makum, slowly, menacingly. Makum breathed in fire again from his torch and blew it in a torrent toward Dayud. It merged with the flame coming toward him, the flames consuming each other, then spiriting back toward Dayud.

Dayud, the muscles in his face trembling with anger and fury, threw the giant flame back to Makum with his hands outstretched and one word, "Caxum!"

Before it reached Makum, Makum breathed in a third flame and again blew it in a plume at Dayud. It joined the attacking giant flame, growing even larger in its midair suspension, almost reaching the cave ceiling.

Suddenly, Dayud ran at the flame, pushing it forward ahead of him toward Makum. Makum breathed in a fourth flame, but in a flash, the massive flame reached him, joining with the torch, consuming him in a giant combustion. The fiery Makum ran into the tunnel out of the cave, Dayud chasing after him.

"Now, Edora. Return to your body. I will keep watch, but you must do what you can. Dayud is greatly weakened by his magic with Makum and with his anger. This will give you advantage, but be wary, he is a danger."

"Yes, Jaxper. I will do what I must. I will do what I can."

In an instant, she was back on the cave floor. The firefighting had increased the temperature in the cave to a nearly intolerable level. She could breathe easier down low near the floor, but her body was also still numb from whatever herbs Dayud was burning.

She stayed low, waiting for her body's strength to increase enough to stand. Waiting for Dayud's return, she rehearsed her magick in her head, repeating the chants, repeating the mind-swell, building them to a crescendo so loud, she could hear them echo silently throughout her body. It had an unexpected effect. Her body shook off its drugged delirium and Edora could feel her energy spike into a heady rush.

Dayud returned, storming toward Edora's body. He kicked at something and Edora heard stones crash against other stones. Not wanting to give away her renewed spirit, she didn't dare open her eyes to see what was happening.

Dayud continued kicking at stones, Edora guessed by the sounds. He raged in a giant roar and Edora could feel the heat of the bonfire increase and lick her side. She steadied her focus and tried to stay open to Jaxper at the same time, splitting her mind in two. She heard Dayud walking away from her, continuing to strike anything in his path. After several minutes of silence, she heard him approaching again. He was circling the bonfire. For what reason she didn't know, but she listened carefully as the sounds of him walking away and nearing from the other side occurred again.

On his third round when Dayud must've been about half-way around the bonfire, Edora heard Jaxper's voice in her head: *Now, Edora.*

Edora breathed in deeply and stood, looking around to gain her bearings. She was hidden from Dayud's sight momentarily as the fire was solidly between them and large enough to conceal her frame. She began walking in the same direction as Dayud in order to continue to hide until he realized she wasn't on the ground anymore.

It only took about 15 strides and Dayud roared again and the bonfire doubled in size, "Edora! You cannot escape me! My fire will devour you."

Edora took a step back from the heat but continued walking as she sensed he had done the same. Then she started to run, again as she sensed he had.

He bellowed again and the bonfire tripled in size. She increased her distance from the heat and continued running. She stopped suddenly. She knew he had too. Somehow, she could sync with his motions, his thoughts.

Above the volume of the fire's crackling, she heard incantations. The fire was now dancing in patterned waves she could discern as she peered closely, much like the patterned waves of water when she scried. She tried to read them but then, in an instant, she was surrounded by flames. Edora's moment had come. She ignored the heat, the panic, the urge to run through them to escape. Standing as still and calm as if nothing at all could harm her, she called down water from the heavens. "Water, be here now. Water surround me. Water become me. Water protect me. Water consume all fire."

She saw water emerge from nothing up above her and come down and around her, she became one with it and in an instant, like blowing out a candle, the bonfire was gone. Edora stood wet and shaking, searching for Dayud.

He stood at the opposite end of the cave. His cloak, his dark hair, had all the signs that he was as drenched as Edora was.

"How? How? How have you defeated fire? How have you defeated me?" He ran at her, but she stood her ground. Calling water again in a waterfall of cascading torrent that kept him from drawing near. The strength of it would have pounded him into the floor. She could sense his growing rage and felt him pull forth his fire energy to combat her water energy. The battle was not over. Not by far. It had only just begun.

Chapter Twenty

The King woke from a fevered dream, feeling like he was drowning in a giant wave of hot water. He shook his head trying to clear the images from his memory. Breathing deeply, he waited for his panic to calm and then got up and paced around the inside of his tent, hoping the dream was not an omen of impending doom. Whatever it was, he was unable to return to sleep. He rested back on his makeshift cot, assembled only for him as King, and rehearsed the actions he knew they must take that night after a long day of riding. Apprehension filled his body again. He had to gain control of his fear if he was to lead them to victory. By the morrow, he would either be victorious or defeated. Tomorrow he would save Devor or he would fail, and the kingdom-city would fall. If by sheer will alone he could prevent it, Devor was already saved. He knew, though, that it would take much more than sheer will to overcome so great a foe as he had seen. The luck of the heavens, whether their attack surprised enough to gain advantage, and whether his oracular vision was accurate would have more to do with the outcome than his force of will. The sorcerer was too powerful to think otherwise.

His thoughts turned to even more dangerous territory. Was Edora alive? Was Edora safe? His thoughts roamed, imagining torture and beatings.

To stop his own thoughts from paralyzing him with anxiety, he stood back up and got dressed for the day, two hours before sunrise. He stepped outside the tent, gave the lookout a nod to affirm his well-being, and strode around the campfire, circling it, gaining strength from it, refusing to bow to the fear of death by fire.

Makum awoke, his skin burning, his throat parched. Where was he? All was dark.

He tried to roll over to get up, but attempting to do so caused more pain than he had ever experienced in his body in his life. He remembered the cries of a child whose father beat him to within a breath of death. This was far more excruciating than that. A scream tried to escape his throat, but the lack of moisture made his vocalization an empty wind. His tongue thick, it stuck to the roof of his mouth. He wished he could die. He willed himself to die. He fell back into a dark unconsciousness.

The city of Devor was a hive of activity. Everywhere one looked, people conveyed pots of water, while talking to neighbors and helping those who were too frail to heed the alert to store five days water for every household and all livestock from the city's cisterns. Even children were running with small pails slopping water over their sides, as all who could worked to fortify their beloved city and follow the King's command. They functioned like a military force—with meticulous order and coordination—all overseen by the General's second-in-command. By the first day's end, they had stored most of what they needed. Tomorrow they would finish and be ready to withstand a five-day siege on their city's water supply.

In the meantime, the river Bedoga flowed on, undisturbed by human hands.

The King's troop was ready by dawn. After eating and prepping their horses, they started off at a slow trot, then increased speed gradually to help their steeds warm up. The King had mapped out their journey with the General in the hour before dawn, when the King couldn't tolerate being the only one up, other than the lookout. They prepped their plan of approach and their strategy for attack, accounting for as many variables that they could anticipate. What if the sorcerer's men knew they were coming? What if the Bedoga river had already been diverted and they were too late? What if the sorcerer was already there? What if Edora was a bargaining chip used by the sorcerer to manipulate them?

They strategized the best they could coming up with alternative tactics for each of these scenarios, but really the King felt his oracular vision had given them their strongest advantage: approach at dark by the second day, when they were most vulnerable. Making secondary plans was wise, but he knew unnecessary if his vision was accurate. He had to trust. He had no other choice.

He would know soon enough if he was wise or foolish to do so.

Dayud's fireball tore through Edora's waterfall. Edora ducked to miss it, but behind the fireball came a surprise. In flew Dayud in the form of a large raven. Just before he attacked her with talons outstretched towards her face, Edora reclaimed the water, surrounding herself with a spinning ball of water. The raven squawked and fell to the cave's floor by the rush of water. Edora could feel Dayud become human again, even though the water surrounding her blinded her from seeing him directly. With more incantations, Dayud conjured his fire energy.

Edora knew he would again lob a fireball at her as it was effective the last time. This time, though, she was prepared. She became the water. Her body flowed with water. She was water. And Dayud's fireball shot straight through the ball of water that was now Edora. It was a strange sensation, she thought. It was like very warm water passing right through her momentarily and then it was gone.

Dayud screamed. He lobbed another fireball and another. They all passed through Edora, the water seer, the water witch. He tried to grab her, but his hand went right through her. Edora thought peacefully to herself, *Of course, how do you hold on to flowing water?* He then surrounded her water orb with fire, but it did nothing to disturb or impede the flow of water in her or around her. It simply warmed the water. Edora found she could even control the temperature of the water if it got too hot by slowing down the water molecules that she herself was.

Edora had won. She knew it and she knew Dayud knew it. He held no more power over her here.

Sensing the futility of wasting any more of his energy, Dayud fled the cave. He would have to fight Devor without her and gain victory from beneath her. He was humiliated. But this made him angrier than he had ever felt before. Tasting metal in his mouth, he knew he had to strengthen himself before he attempted his conquest of Devor. Edora may have won a battle but he would still be victorious over Devor, and without Devor, Edora was stripped of her power over him. She could do nothing to him outside of its walls. He could reign freely from within and he knew she would be unable to impede his ever-growing realm.

Dayud grabbed at food stores he had kept in the pack on his steed. He ate and drank greedily, trying to restore some of his energy in this most base way, even though crude for a sorcerer. Then he swung up onto his horse and sped away, hoping to find that his men were ready for the first stage of Devor's defeat. If Edora died in this barren location with no food and no transport, all the better. He didn't need her. He'd been a fool to think so. Now he knew. His drive to prove that he could master anyone whose element was water almost proved to be his downfall. He didn't need to prove it. It was another futile task his old master had weakened his mind on. He had really believed that without mastering water, he would be vulnerable. If he had not believed it, he would not have put himself in this weakening situation. He might already have Devor by siege. But no matter, now he was wise to his true power. Edora was abandoned and he would be victorious.

Edora remained one with the water until she felt Dayud's presence leave. The water seemed to enhance her already highly perceptive gifts, and she was aware of Dayud's intent without his presence near her or without seeing it through her gift of sight. It was a new experience for her, but with Jaxper's tutelage, she had fully mastered water when she needed it the most. Now that Dayud was gone, she relinquished her mind's focus on oneness with water. The water aura around her splashed onto the cave floor, and Edora's body gelled and then solidified. It was strange being back inside a solid body again. The bonfire was nowhere to be seen. Edora could barely see by the light of just a few torches still lit and circling the caveroom. Some must have been doused in the cascading waterfalls.

Jaxper's words floated into her awareness, *Well done, Edora. You mastered water AND you defeated Dayud. You learn fast.* He ended his words with his predictable chuckle.

Thanks to you, Edora thought back to him. *I never would have defeated him without your lessons on water. I didn't know if I'd be able to do it in the moment, but it came easier when I was at risk for my life. Thank you, thank you, Jaxper. What ever can I do to repay you?*

No repayment necessary. As I told you, this was my life's work, to prepare you for this moment, Jaxper added.

Well the moment has come and gone. What do I do now? I don't have any way out of here and although I can conjure up water, I doubt there are food stores here. Edora thought more to herself than to Jaxper. Nevertheless, he answered in kind.

True. True. But the man who fled here in flame? Makum? His horsey is wandering. He rode off on him after dowsing Dayud's flames by rolling in sand. However, the pain from his burns was too much and he couldn't get back on his horsey. I'll see what I can do to coax the horsey toward the cave. Go looking for him in a few minutes. Rest for now. You still have work to do.

Jaxper's telepathy went silent and Edora realized she was exhausted. She sat down on a boulder that was situated at the edge of what had been the bonfire. It was invitingly warm, but its rough edges were none-too-comfortable. However, it was the most suitable for supporting her. She bent over and put her head in her hands and her head between her legs. It was the end of one battle but not the end.

Jaxper was right. She still had work to do to help save Devor. She tried to see in her mind's eye what might befall her King and his mighty kingdom-city, but nothing came—a first. She must be more spent than even she realized. She had survived. She was okay. First, she needed to leave and find some nourishment.

Slowly she stood and gained her feet. Stretching, she felt her joints find their positions and her sinews find their lengths again. She breathed in deeply and tried a step and then another. She was stable, her footing sure. She kept moving—slowly, toward the cave's dark entrance. As she walked through the dark tunnel, she felt a rebirthing— a re-entrance into the watery womb from which she had come from her dear mamá. She had entered this cave, a water seer and was leaving a water master. She had gone from using water to becoming water. She would be different in the world. She felt less like she was subject to the whims of the destiny of others around her, more like she was a part of the natural order of life itself. Not penetrable. Not impenetrable. Pan penetrable. In all. With all. Part of all. There was nothing to be overcome. There was nothing to overcome. There was only all in all and she a part of whatever the all was. All-overcoming.

The King raced his troop toward their goal—the General right behind him. They took turns driving their horses ahead interspersed with cool-downs and slow trots. Their steeds were well-bred and accustomed to riding in the wilds. This was the most barren and wildest terrain they had ever traveled, and the King didn't want to drive them to their limit. There were too many uncertainties, too many variables to account for. They needed to be able to flee over a long distance at a moment's notice. So, the horses had to be well-rested by the time they reached their destination at nightfall.

They were close. Far off in the distance, as night was slowly descending like a lazy theatre curtain after the day's act, the King espied a winding path of trees. Signaling that a river was nearby that watered the roots of the only trees they had seen for miles, the King slowed the troop gradually until they were walking the horses. From their maps and sundial compasses they'd determined to arrive at the river south of the point of contact, so that the shield of trees and the cover of darkness would be their best disguise.

Just before reaching the line of trees, General Morlay ordered a stop. Gathering together the troop on horses, the General motioned them even closer. A horse whinnied and started to buck. Too close. Its rider took the horse out of the circle for space and to keep it quiet.

"We have arrived. Tonight we make our move. If our intelligence is correct…"—he looked over at the King knowing full well that the intelligence was not at all verifiable—"…they will be encamped at the intersection of rivers Cressic and Bedoga. Their plan is to divert the river that runs through Devor to create panic and loss of essential life-giving water. This is a moment of significant weakness for them. They do not know we are here. They do not know that we have wells to withstand a siege. They do not know that Devor is already prepared for a siege. They do not have honor. We will be victorious.

"It is possible they hold the King's"—here he searched for the right word to use—"*advisor* as captive, as ransom. It is not possible to know. If this is the case, we will retreat and not negotiate for her release. Neither will we yield Devor. The revelation of our presence should be enough to forestall any attack on Devor, knowing that we are aware of and ready for their plan."

The General went on discussing strategy with different options and outcomes, depending on what they might encounter. Answering questions for the better part of an hour, they dismounted to prepare for attack. Eating lightly, and feeding and watering horses took the better part of another hour. By then, two scouts had returned.

"The men we seek are about five miles northwest of here as the river winds. They are asleep in camp save for one lookout. A small company, we match them in numbers. If the sorcerer is there, we cannot ascertain. It appeared their diversion of the river is nearing completion. We are right to arrive now."

The General and the King conferred quietly with this news and after the General announced, "We will make haste then in one-half hour, during the darkest of the night, and while the guard is light. Arm up. We will pursue the operation dark.

The troop mounted their steeds, heading off north riding next to the line of trees.

As they approached their target, a bowman took up position ahead of the troop and let an arrow fly toward their lookout near the bonfire. He had his back to them. An easy target. The arrow met its mark, the man went down silently, and the troop circled the encampment.

A rider slid off her horse. She was small and had the gift of stealth. She stole into the camp as silently as a feather landing on a cloud, and lighted her torch from the single bonfire at the center of camp. Moving away quickly she made her way back to the troop, lighting another torch held by one of the riders at the front. He then passed the flame along in both directions to the riders beside him in the circle. These shared their flames with riders at their sides, until all of the riders at the front held fiery torches aloft. At a single hand motion from the General, each of these flame-bearing riders started forward. As they reached an inner tent, they set it on fire. Retreating they set the outer tents on fire, creating walls of inferno to trap the men inside.

If any tried to escape, Devor's soldiers had bows and swords ready to take them down one at a time. It was over in a matter of a few minutes. Few escaped and they were ambushed at once.

General Morlay let the tents burn to the ground, taking care not to let the fire spread to any nearby brush or trees. Being that the enemy encampment was close to the rivers' juncture, the troop regathered by the trench while the remains smoldered. Then they started the arduous task of shoveling—filling back in the trench that was to be used to divert the river Bedoga into the Cressic. They worked for hours until the dawn. Because they wanted to leave by the morning light, they were unable to complete the task. It would've taken them

159

days to fill it all back in, but it was enough to stop any one or even two men from completing the diversion themselves. It would hold until after the completion of whatever siege the sorcerer laid on Devor.

As they left the Bedoga river mostly intact, they retreated for several miles back to their original line of contact with the river. From there they would scout to confirm no more enemies presented themselves to work on the Bedoga river's diversion and also to keep an eye out for the sorcerer.

It had been too easy. There had been almost no fight. No threat.

"Let's rest until the morn of tomorrow, and if there is no more sign of the enemy, let us make haste back to Devor. I want to ensure that it is not left to itself in case of a devious plan by the sorcerer. It was too easy to defeat his men to give me rest," the King stated to his General.

"It leaves me uneasy as well. I thought we'd encounter some resistance, but they were completely unprepared. Where is the sorcerer I wonder? I do not believe he was among them tonight."

"No, I do not believe he was. He has an affinity for fire. He can transform. He would have made himself known and visible if he were here."

General Morlay scoffed to himself inside, but then remembered the testimony of the castle guard. "Do you think the sorcerer has Edora? There is no sign she was here either." The General and his troop had scoured the ashes, retrieving swords, metal coins, and searching for any signs of identification.

"I hope not, but it is odd that both are missing from the equation tonight. Nevertheless, our priority is securing Devor. Now that we have strengthened the banks of the river adequately enough for now, we must return as soon as we can confirm that the enemy camp is demolished without unknown reinforcements appearing."

The General was again glad the King's priority was on securing Devor and not on searching for Edora. They had no way to know where she was or even if she were alive. He had to give the King even more credit. The enemy encampment had been vulnerable exactly during the time he had foreseen. The King had said it was only to be vulnerable for two days. What that meant he didn't know, but clearly the King wanted to extend their stay for the full two days to make sure that the camp's vulnerability wasn't ending due to new enemy troops on the way or some other complication.

They rotated scouts every two hours until the following morning. They saw nothing out of the ordinary and so with the last scout's retreat, they hastened back to Devor to secure their kingdom-city.

If they would have stayed for two more hours, scouts would have witnessed someone appear in the burned-out encampment.

Chapter Twenty-One

Edora made her way through the cave's dark entrance out into the light. She had no idea an entire day had passed and was surprised it was the next morning that greeted her. She had thought late afternoon or evening would find her. No wonder she was hungry. She wandered a bit in the bright morning sun, not really sure where she was going to find that ride.

Walking around the side of the mountain to the east, near the rocks she spotted a horse, saddled, yet alone. This must be the one Jaxper had mentioned. She approached the roan steed cautiously, not wanting to startle it into running away.

"Hello, there. How are you this morning? Are you looking for some food? I am too. How about we join up?" Edora talked softly to the horse who looked at her warily but did not bolt.

She stepped beside him, taking the reins to keep a hold on him, and then reached into the saddlebags. Inside one there was moldy bread and cheese but also an apple that hadn't yet met its bag-mates' fate. Edora took a few bites of the apple and then held out the rest for the horse to eat off her open hand. She found a water pouch on the other saddle bag and some dried meat jerky. She took a few bites of the jerky but didn't like the taste. It wasn't much to help satisfy her hunger, but it would have to do. More importantly, she had to find a way to get the horse some water. She drunk deeply of the water pouch, quenching her own thirst, and looked around for anything that could hold some water for a horse.

Eventually, Edora found a rock whose top was caved in like a shallow bowl. Pouring the rest of the water pouch onto the rock, she again became the water witch, causing the water not only to stir, but to multiply.

The horse, who was quite amenable to her now, drank almost all of what the rock could hold. Edora again multiplied the waters until the horse was satisfied with its drink.

Using the stirrup, she gathered herself up onto her ride and off they trotted. Edora knew where the encampment was from which she had come, but wanting to avoid that route, she headed north to go around Travessa in the familiar route. She took it slow, both for her ride and for herself.

Dayud gathered the speed of his own horse under him as he flew toward the encampment. His men should be ready to dam and divert the river Bedoga away from Devor. Then they would ride to Devor, waiting until the King's troops left to investigate the dammed-up river. They would attack while Devor was without water and with their best soldiers away.

He was less than an hour away from their encampment. Weakened from the battle with Edora, yet his anger burned in him still. His internal fire was immense and strong. He would be victorious. It was only a matter of time and power.

Edora found her way to Travessa and then she made her way south back to the village, Javenia, where she had first encountered Jaxper. He was there waiting for her in the market square, just as he had the first time. It was midday of the next day. Edora had camped beside the Bedoga river overnight.

"Glad you're here, dearie. I've got food on. Let's make our way quickly. We don't want to raise suspicions." Jaxper warned.

"Suspicions? That doesn't sound very heartening. You don't normally talk like that," Edora questioned him.

"Aye, aye. There's something afoot I can't quite tell. Let's get back to home where we'll be safe and sound." Jaxper looked around behind him nervously, like he was about to get attacked at any moment.

Edora dismounted her ride and led the horse on the trail as she followed Jaxper, feeling quite uneasy herself. She had never seen Jaxper this wary—even when he said goodbye to her as she left to confront Dayud. Jaxper was chipper by nature. Fear didn't suit him well. She wondered what would transpire next, that might be even worse than what she'd already endured.

The troop arrived back at Devor, weary in body but full of the energy of victory. King Beon wasted no time, not wanting to rest until he was sure of the sorcerer's full defeat. He had no more oracular vision guiding him now, nor Edora. He was operating on instinct alone and he knew while a powerful sorcerer still bent his will against them, danger was present. He ordered the General to ascertain the status of their reserves and to reinforce their defenses.

General Morlay left the King and started executing his orders, putting more scouts out beyond the normal perimeter. He made the rounds, checking in with his next-in-commands and taking their reports of what had transpired in the troop's absence. He then added more soldiers to the perimeter walls, giving short commands to keep all of his troops' spirits up.

"We defeated them at their deceit. We'll defeat them again. Heads up. Stay alert. Victory is ours for our enemy has no honor. Anything that's amiss, report it at once."

While the General rallied his troops, the King withdrew to his private chambers to eat and retire his travel wear. Reclad in his royal attire, he laid out a map of Devor on his chamber table. He scanned it for any sign of weakness, any point that was vulnerable that could be breached. Seeing none, he sat back in his chair, and sighed. Closing his eyes, he thought through all that he knew about the sorcerer.

What would the sorcerer do when he saw what had become of his men and camp? Was the sorcerer even alive? He sensed that yes, he was. He knew the sorcerer was sly, able to transform, conniving for months to find Edora. Why? Why was Edora his target? The answer eluded him the more he pondered it. There were pieces of this puzzle that he did not have. Would his scribe know? Probably not. His scribe had been used unwittingly.

What then? What was the sorcerer's ultimate goal? Power. All men like him craved power. Why then go after Edora? Did she have power that he did not have? Did he need her? Did he need her out of the way to gain Devor? Maybe both were true. She was now out of the way. Did he have her so he could use her against Devor? This was the King's main fear, but he had to leave his personal feelings aside. How could the sorcerer use Edora against Devor?

Really, Edora knew very little about the workings of Devor. She had existed in an isolated, sheltered room in their kingdom-city. Everything she knew, she knew through her gifts. She would never betray Devor through her gifts, not if she held breath. That he knew. But would anyone else believe this? And could the sorcerer use his devilry to overcome and manipulate an innocent soul? Could Edora withstand his powers?

Was Edora even alive? His mind was circling now over thoughts that had been running in loops since Edora had left. He wasn't getting anywhere. It was pointless to ruminate on things he had no way to verify, on matters he had no information on. The last time he'd been caught up in these worries, he'd had an oracular vision. None was forthcoming this time.

The King rolled up the map, got up and stored it, and left his lunch, largely uneaten. He couldn't stomach the thought of spending time eating so much good food when there was much to be done and insufficient time to savor the goodness.

King Beon ordered his Royal Guard to its highest alert. No one got in or out of the castle except by royal decree. He left his own Tower and circled the outer grounds, encouraging his citizens, helping them prepare for what could be another onslaught of fire. This time they were ready. Having saved the river, at least for now, and with many days' supply of water and food, they were watering down roofs and anything that could burn to prevent the destruction the last attack had brought.

The action helped ease the King's gnawing disquiet. The more he moved, the freer he felt. The freer he felt, the greater his sense of coming victory. Yet in his muted euphoria, he steadied his heart. He knew there would be a certain amount of damage he could not control.

Dayud erupted as the sight of his burned encampment came into view. Screaming in rage, he spun his mount around, trying to clear his head from what he thought must be an illusion, a trick of the mind, a mirage from his enemies.

Completing his revolution, he raced toward the charred ruins and remains, seeing that nothing and no one was left. He would not believe it. His men could not have been wiped out. They were the best warriors he knew. He had trained them in stealth and combat and fire weaponry. How did they fall? He had no one left. No one! He sped off to the banks of the rivers to see if at least his primary scheme had prevailed.

It had not. The banks were weakly but largely restored. His nearly eternal fury was kindled then into a darker place, beyond the flame of revenge. Molten hot, burning beyond fire, it reshaped his inner landscape. No longer would his thirst be sated with victory. His lust for power twisted in upon itself. He didn't want to rule the world. He meant to destroy it.

But first, he must ruin those who had brought this destruction on him. The King of Devor was his priority and Edora next if she had not already wasted away from starvation by the time he was done with the King and all of Devor.

He galloped off on a straight trajectory towards the great kingdom-city. He planned to use their weakest link against them.

Back in Jaxper's cottage, Edora ate and drank her fill, then collapsed in uninterrupted sleep on the reclining bench in the front room. She dreamt of fire and water, of earth and wind. Her mamá floated on the clouds, her papá slept deep in the earth. From the surface of the earth, several strands of clay arose in spiraling stalks, climbing all the way to the clouds. Her mamá grabbed on to one of the clay stalks and it reversed its direction bringing her down to the surface of the earth. But she was still separated from her love, far below the surface.

Her mamá bent down over the surface of the earth and wept bitter tears of sorrow. The tears watered the surface, creating a large, wild lake. The lake reached so deeply and saturated the earth so fully that drops started to fall on her papá's face deep in the earth and it woke him from his slumber. He reached out his hand to the top of the pocket of earth he lay in. Feeling moist dirt, he dug with his fingers through the mud, until a wave of water rushed in and filled his little earth pocket. He kept digging until he could swim out, and up and up he swam to the lake's surface. Seeing her love in the middle of the lake of tears, Edora's mamá rejoiced and swam to him where they embraced and floated together, arm in arm, the waves happily tossing them till they reached shore wedded together.

Edora awoke from her dream, grieving and fevered. She missed her parents so much. Sobbing, she mopped up her tears with a blanket Jaxper must have thrown over her while she slept. Her body was burning up. Was she getting sick? Now was not a good time for a flu. There was more work she had to do although she had no idea what it was. She'd beaten Dayud face-to-face and one-on-one. Jaxper was sure Dayud was up to something even he was afraid of. What could it be?

She thanked her dear mamá and papá for coming to her in a dream, bittersweet and mournful as it was for her. It meant to her that they were together in the afterlife, what her mamá always referred to as "the bliss." Throwing off the damp blanket, which was suffocating her in her fevered state, she stood up and called for Jaxper. He didn't appear.

"Jaxper, where are you?"

She looked everywhere in the cottage but couldn't find him. Sweat was pouring off of her dangerously hot skin. Something was wrong, but she didn't know what. Was this a side effect from defeating the element of fire? Was she being attacked? Was Dayud behind this?

She wandered around outside, calling for Jaxper. She saw him finally out by the horses, feeding and tending them. Then everything went dark.

Chapter Twenty-Two

Havorth, the scribe, was beyond his own coping. His house arrest was a torture beyond torture. Happy his home had been spared during the firestorm and grateful his lover—former lover—had not seemed to be targeting him specifically, yet all day and all night, day after day, he paced, he read, he ate, and he slept. No one visited. No one checked on him. He was betrayed by his people. Forgotten. Tossed aside. He didn't know how much longer he could go on with no duties, no purpose. He felt his mind unraveling—the threads that kept his fine thinking in order were tearing, shredding, disintegrating.

He was sure the King was busy, what with the fire attack and then the sudden storing of water by everyone, there was clearly something else brewing. He hated being out of the inner circle, especially having been at the center of that royal loop for years. He spat into the spittoon beside his writing table. Why couldn't the King give him any news? Oh, right. Because if he knew anything, his former lover might force the information out of him again.

How? How had Stavon—if that was even his lover's real name—done it? He had absolutely no memory of being coerced or manipulated into revealing information. They had never even discussed anything remotely connected to his work, well, except that he was the King's scribe. It ended there.

He scoffed at the idea that Stavon was a sorcerer. Who believed such nonsense in today's world? Sorcery was for children's stories and superstitious, uneducated people. But, the raven. The raven! The image of that raven flew into his mind just as quickly and shockingly as it had flown by him that treacherous day. It had been Stavon. He knew it, even though it forced him to consider that Stavon was, in fact, a sorcerer.

"NO! It cannot be!" Havorth yelled at no one and everyone, emphasizing his exclamation with a single loud bang on the wooden table by his closed fist.

Pounding on Havorth's front and only wooden door commenced a fraction of a second later. "Is everything all right in there, Mr. Pentimult?"

Havorth responded testily back to the guard at the door, "Yes, yes. I'm fine. Just a little frustration from being cooped up in here all the time. I'm fine. Go back to your guarding." He uttered "guarding" with as much loathing as his tongue could spew. Guarding was an occupation so beneath his high estate, he held no esteem for it. The irony that he had been the white lady's true guard escaped him.

Havorth looked out the back window of his cottage. People were still bustling around, busy with errands and personal affairs, walking at a desperate pace. Devor was on the cusp of something urgent. Even if it was devastation, he wished it would hurry before he died of boredom or came apart from torment.

Edora startled awake to find Jaxper standing over her, looking at her with a quizzical eye. She was back on the reclining bench in Jaxper's sitting room.

"What's wrong?" she asked him.

"You gave me a scare, you did. Collapsing in a fever. I thought maybe I'd put you up to too much. But you're all better now, dearie," Jaxper answered.

"Why did the fever come? Am I ill? Was it the sorcery?" Edora wanted answers.

"I'm not really sure, sweetie. I cast some protective enchantments over you and your fever subsided, so perhaps the sorcery. That Dayud is a clever one. He may have put a permanent curse of fire on you that lasted beyond your battle with him."

"Is that the evil you sensed on my way here?" Edora was feeling much better and significantly less warm with every passing moment.

170

"Perhaps. I'm just glad you walked out to find me. If I didn't get to you then, I'm not sure what would've happened." A small tear slid down Jaxper's face. "I'm sorry I wasn't watching over you more carefully. That was my error. I'm sorry, dearie."

"Oh, Jaxper. I know you've done everything you could. I'm fine now. I've been in danger for a long time. That's not going away anytime soon, I imagine. Not until Dayud is defeated once and for all. Do you have more food? I'm suddenly very hungry again."

Jaxper chuckled and left for the kitchen, bringing back heaps of bread, cheese, soup, and a tonic tea. Edora felt badly that he had worried over her. He had done so much. He couldn't know everything that would happen. He couldn't protect her from everything, either.

She wondered that she didn't have any memories of him from childhood. What he had told her mesmerized her. How had she not known? Of course, her parents had kept knowledge of him from her out of necessity. Still, according to Jaxper, they had spent a lot of time together. Perhaps the trauma of having to flee their home village and country had obliterated a lot of her childhood memories.

According to Jaxper, life was idyllic in their home village of Banizar. Love and family were plentiful. She played with other children and she helped her parents with their industries as only a child could—sometimes reliably, sometimes not. Her father's industry was woodworking, her mother's second sight. They weren't wealthy but they had plenty and enjoyed wide support for their goodwill. Jaxper was her mother's elder brother. He lived in the same village and had a similar family gift of second sight. He had travelled far while young, learning magic—a luxury young men were granted, young women were not. Although her mamá had wanted to travel and learn too, her parents forbade it. When Jaxper returned after a decade away, he taught everything he knew to his younger sister, Edora's mamá, in secret.

On the eve of the day Edora was born, Jaxper was given a vision. This time he was to go away for good. He was to practice his trade in a faraway country and wait, for a time would come in the far-off future that he would need to save his niece and his sister's family line from a terrible fate. His work would help thousands.

And so, in time, when Edora was still very young, Jaxper left. Edora's mamá and family were heartbroken, afraid they would never see him again. Jaxper made them swear they would not follow him and that they would not talk about him to anyone. He wanted to be forgotten.

It devastated them. Jaxper could not tell them why he had to leave. Telling them could fracture the path Edora was on. Everything needed to unfold naturally without intervention—until the right time. And so, he left for good, leaving everyone he loved and knew behind, with them thinking that he left because he wanted to leave them.

Jaxper had traveled for years, settling in different villages and countries, throughout the Centric Lands and eventually received the oracular vision to come to the village of Javenia and await further instruction. This was a mere two years ago. He settled in a little, abandoned cottage that had been forgotten by the village. He lived there undisturbed, until he received the vision he had been waiting to receive for thirty-three years. Edora would be arriving the next day. He tidied his cottage, left in the early morning in case she was herself early, and busied himself around the village square without being seen.

He knew her as soon as he saw her. She looked the same, just all grown-up. White blonde hair, fair skin. She stuck out in this country like any of her kin and country would. Jaxper himself had similar traits, but with time, his towhead had become gray. He stood out even less now with his grayed hair mostly gone and a bald dome in its place. And his face and skin aged with lines, made him even less suspicious as a foreigner. Who would bother with a wrinkled man, bent over, who chuckled a lot? He appeared harmless and he liked it that way.

In the few days they had together before Edora faced Dayud, he had taught her how to use her natural affinity for water to defeat fire. This was his life's task. He would help her to defeat the sorcerer.

And they had. Edora and her uncle, Jaxper, had defeated Dayud together. For the time being.

But now it was Jaxper's turns for questions. When she had devoured everything that he had placed in front of her to eat, he set his mind toward understanding why exactly Dayud was so keen to destroy Edora. The answers escaped his vision for some reason, but he could see that Edora now knew who Dayud was.

"Edora, would you mind telling me everything you know about Dayud? I could see you recognized him when you saw him face to face, but I'm afraid I can't quite put the pieces together. It had something to do with our family?"

Edora was surprised at the question. She realized she'd ascribed omniscience to her uncle—he seemed to know everything—but now she was the one with the inside information.

Edora cleared her throat and pushed back from the little round table she'd been eating at with Jaxper.

"I'm sure I don't have all the details. What mamá related to me was assuredly filtered to protect me as a child. But she couldn't protect me from what happened to us. This is what I know.

"Mamá, as you know, was a gifted seer who helped our villagers with prophecies and healings. We were well-respected. I loved playing with the village children, my friends. One day, mamá gave a prophecy to the wealthiest family of our village. You might remember them, the Stallexi?"

Edora waited and Jaxper nodded a yes.

"The father was part of the King's council and very influential. The mother came to mamá one day as her eldest son was sick, though

173

she did not tell mamá this. She asked only for a prophesy. I was outside playing as usual, with the younger son and daughters along with some other village children.

"When the mother came out of her tent, she was very upset and took her son and daughters away abruptly. I knew something was wrong and went inside our little cottage. Mamá didn't look well. She had her talismans spread out on her drawing table and her face was pallid. All the light had gone out of it.

'What's wrong, Mamá?' I asked her.

'Nothing to worry about. You run along and play,' she advised me.

"But I knew something was very wrong. I could see it on her face and in her eyes and in the mother's eyes when she left our cabin.

"A few days later, we heard that the family's eldest son had died. Mamá was beside herself. Papá tried to comfort her and ease her mind, but she wouldn't have it. She begged him to go to the family with our deepest condolences and with many gifts of sorrow as was the custom.

"He did as she asked, bringing food, woodcrafts from his shop, and healing herbs from mamá as tokens of our collective grief. However, papá was not welcomed. In fact, he was chased off their lands.

"Upon hearing this news, mamá was stricken with a foreboding vision. She began packing and storing our wares. Papá was trying to calm her, telling her to give it time. All would settle down."

"That very evening, our neighbors knocked on our door and warned us that the Stallexi family had told everyone that mamá had cursed their son and killed him. They would seek their vengeance.

"And so, in the dead of night, we set out on foot, to give some distance and time away from the village and the family. However, the family's hired men had already made chase. They caught up with us near the next village. Papá heard them coming and sent us on ahead into the village to a friend who sheltered us. Papá stayed and confronted the men, trying to fight them off single-handedly and was killed. They looked for mamá and me but could not find us. Our friends sheltered us for two more nights in the food cellar below ground. We fled when we were told the men had moved on to a different village, believing papá and mamá had split up and gone in separate directions to throw them off mamá's path.

"We fled from village to village for years, always wondering if death was just around the corner. Mamá's gift of sight helped us stay ahead of their ever-threatening chase and helped us fund our food and shelter with trades of healing and insight.

"Eventually we settled in a barn in a village south of Devor, trading in and around the streets of Devor. It was after a year there that mamá was killed when our barn caught fire and the smoke ruined her lungs. She died…"

Edora caught herself. She was choking, gagging, remembering the thick smoke and the fear of burning to death before the smoke could kill her and her dear mamá. Tears welled up in her eyes as she felt again the suffering of her mamá's last few weeks as her lungs gradually failed her. She looked up at Jaxper and he too was crying.

He spoke softly, "I lost my family long ago by my Spirits when I left. I never saw my sister, your mamá, or my parents again. I knew my parents had died soon after I left. I had learned that much on my own through gossip and divining. An odd combination, I know, but truth travels fast and in many ways," he gave a chuckle, but a humorless one this time. "And now I have just found out how my sister and her husband were lost. Now I know why I had to leave. I needed to leave long before this assault on my sister's family so that I'd be forgotten, never remembered, never chased. I would be safe and hence free to help you and save a great many people."

Edora nodded. Her heart, even in this grievous sadness that often consumed her whenever she thought of her very good mamá and papá, was healing. It was good to be with family, to share in her grief with someone who understood, even if she didn't remember him. He knew her as a child, and he knew her mamá and papá. He too had lost them. Shared grief was easier to carry, she was learning. Finally, she had someone to share it with after bearing it alone for many years. Edora was learning more about Jaxper, too. He was human. He wasn't invincible. He wasn't omniscient. He didn't know all. After she first met him and learned who we was and what he could do, she'd elevated him to practically a god—what her parents had been to her as a child and then some. That was a mistake she wouldn't make again. He was her elder and teacher and uncle, but he didn't know everything. He was about to learn something even more shocking.

Dayud had made it near Devor. He was hiding in a glade beyond the Shandar that had not burned out. It lay to the northwest of the great kingdom-city, beyond the Bedoga. He planned to conserve and even expand his energy. After being completely depleted two days ago, he would need all of his strength now. All of it. No. More than he had ever demonstrated before. He began making a small fire in the center of the glade. Smokeless, below grade, it could never be detected. He had to become the fire, just as Edora had become the water. Chanting an incantation, Dayud performed an intricate dance into the night around the small fire. If anyone had watched, they would have seen fire dancing around fire, circling it, merging together and then moving apart. He danced until the remaining embers of the fire merged with his every cell and his every dark intention. It was time.

The King was back in his chambers for the night. He stayed at his desk, writing out strategies and plans. He had thought out every angle of every defensive move they could take against a sorcerer with unknown powers. What offensive moves could they make? He had no idea. What would he do if he were a sorcerer? Something sly. Something unexpected. So why couldn't he think of anything underhanded? He had dealt with battle and wars in honorable ways. Even though war was ugly, there were rules, common understandings that upheld the dignity of the fight. He didn't know how to fight dirty. He'd never needed to. He couldn't even bend his mind to think like that. Was there someone who could? Was there anyone around him who could think like an evil man?

If there were, he didn't know that man. Or woman. Maybe someone else did. But who? His General was more by-the-book than he. His oracle, who could see into minds, was gone, dead? No, gone. That's all he could accept. No more visions had come to him to help him guide his people to safety. He could feel danger was on their doorstep. He knew evil was coming.

He slept little that night, pacing and pondering how best to counter the uncounterable.

Edora steeled herself for what she was about to relate to Jaxper. Maybe the information would help him understand the danger that was still upon them and upon Devor. Maybe knowing this vital information would be the key that would unlock the mystery of Dayud's destructive path.

Sighing and clearing her throat, she spoke forthrightly to Jaxper, "Uncle, you need to know more of what happened. Dayud is directly connected to our family's attack in Banizar."

"He is?" Jaxper was startled out of a rare moment of self-pity for all he had lost. "How?"

"Dayud is the younger son of the Stallexi family. He is the brother of the older son who died so many years ago. I remembered only when I saw him face-to-face. I used to play with all of those children on occasion. Not often, as we lived in the common village and not among the wealthy landowners. But sometimes, when papá or mamá had business with the family, I would accompany them to their estate and play with them.

"The only reasonable explanation is that he was after me as revenge for the death curse on his brother his family blamed on mamá. I don't know all of what happened after we were chased away and papá was killed, but I imagine it wasn't good, whatever it was."

"This is helpful, Edora. The missing piece of the puzzle that could give us insight into defeating Dayud. Are you sure? Is it him?"

"I'm sure. I could never understand the hatred he directed towards me. Remember, at first, he came only for me in Devor. When he couldn't find me, he launched a fire attack on the city. His hatred was personal, vengeful, and I could not find any reason for anyone to hate me so. When I saw his eyes in person, it all became clear. I knew him. He knew me. We had played together as children. His family blamed mamá for his brother's death."

"Let me contemplate this new knowledge. If you feel ready, you could perform a water scrying and see if you get any guidance on future action. It could be most helpful," Jaxper relayed.

Edora nodded. She felt like she could now. Before the battle with Dayud, all she would see was fire anytime she looked inside her mind or did any divining. She'd had to rely on Jaxper's insight— and training. Now, though, she felt stronger and more stable. Food and sleep had restored her, as she was sure, had Jaxper's protective spells and elixirs.

Jaxper left to go to the back of his cottage where he had his own little workshop set up. Really, his entire cottage was his workshop, what with the water magick on display on every available shelf, flat top, and space. Enthralled when she first stepped foot inside, now she was amazed at how normal it all seemed. Jaxper was a master of water. Far beyond Edora. His skills had strengthened her natural affinity for working with this element, but his understanding went preternaturally beyond hers.

Edora decided to try scrying as Jaxper suggested. The possibilities of water containers to use were endless with his omnipresent water magick. She looked around and decided to use the shallow bowl that

178

had drops endlessly falling into it from midair, and yet the bowl never over-filled. The source of the drip midair was also indeterminable.

Now that she had learned some of Jaxper's knowledge, Edora had an idea about how he might have magicked it. She tried to suspend the drops long enough to do some scrying. She was only marginally successful. The rate of dripping slowed but would never slow enough or stop. So, she poked around the sitting room, trying to find the perfect scrying container. She stopped when she spotted a patterned pottery bowl. The water it held was swirling in a whirlpool formation but in the same colors as the pattern on the bowl itself: shades of teal, lilac, and pomegranate all mixing in an eternal eddy, that went nowhere.

She cast her intentions over the bowl, asking to see her future and the future of Devor and King Beon. As her palm hovered above the water, her body trembled from head to toe. She didn't know if she wanted to see what was coming.

Nevertheless, she forced herself to look. Many lives depended on it.

Dayud was ready. He had transformed himself into fire, just as he desired. Nothing could hinder him now. The fire had restored his energy. He knew what he must do.

Edora couldn't believe what she beheld in the water. There before her very eyes she saw a scene unfolding that shook her to her very core. She knew, again, what she must do.

She ran to the back of the cottage and found Jaxper levitating some bowls of water.

"I thought you were meditating," Edora looked at him puzzled.

179

"I am," Jaxper replied. "Did you scry?"

"I did," Edora responded just as tersely.

"And what did you see, my dearie?" Jaxper asked tenderly.

"Terrible things I wish I had not seen."

"It is the bane of all who see. We portend so much good and so much that is terrible. Can you stop what is to come?"

"I do not know. I must try. I could not live with myself if I did not."

"I will journey to Devor this time with you. However, because I am not a fast traveler by horse, you will go on ahead of me to stop the impending doom if you can. I will arrive as quickly as I can to give aid if possible. In the meantime, you need to pack some food and some other stores and be off as swiftly as possible."

"Really, you know this, Jaxper?"

"My meditation did not show me what would happen as your scry did, but it showed me much haste was needed. We will not delay. Let's begin packing now, dearie."

Edora tried not to let fear reach her heart, but it struck like a hammer on a bell anyway, sending ripples of jolting energy through her, over and over again. She hurried through their preparations, wiping tears away whenever she remembered the images that accosted her in the scrying bowl. She determined to change the foreseen future.

Dayud assumed his position outside the city of Devor. He was hidden. No one would see him. Nevertheless, he waited until the cover of darkness to make his move. Alone, he had the advantage of stealth. He had but one chance. If he were to be discovered, his ability to accomplish his purpose would be critically thwarted. He needed every advantage. All of his energy. The next task would consume an extreme amount of his power, and he still had an even greater expenditure required after that. He could not risk having to use any extra energy to deter an accidental interloper or fend off a random attack. As the sky darkened to a charcoal sea, he sped off on foot toward Devor's city walls.

An old woman sitting in her tufted, overstuffed armchair by the window, looked out through the leaded window's elliptical frame and caught sight of a large black bird flying low over Devor's rooftops. She leaned forward. It was late. It was dark. Could she have been mistaken? She'd never seen such a large bird in her life. But the orders had been clear: Report anything unusual at once. She picked up her cane resting beside her chair, creaked into a standing position, and headed toward the door. Once there, she pulled a hand-knit shawl off a wooden peg on the back of the door, threw it over her shoulders—more out of habit and decorum than necessity, and left her home for the nearest sentry post. She hobbled as quickly as she could. It was the latest hour she'd been out in many years.

Havorth startled awake when a hand covered his mouth. He remembered nothing else for many hours.

King Beon slept uneasily after finally convincing himself that some rest would assist his mind with strategy in the morning. A sharp rapping on the inner door of his royal chamber stirred him from his fitful dreams. Reaching for his robe, he pulled himself up to sitting, throwing the robe around his shoulders.

What could be so urgent at this time? Had the sorcerer struck? Why wasn't a word being spoken to announce who was knocking and why? His staff and his General would never break protocol in such an astounding manner.

As the King slipped his feet into the soft leather moccasins set out for him beside his bed for the morning, he called out, "Who's there?"

There was no answer, just more rapid knocking.

Sensing something was highly amiss, he stood but stayed by his bed, pulling his sword from its hilt hidden behind the nightstand.

He waited. Another round of rapping, even more loudly. He wondered if he should betray his continuing presence by questioning whoever was knocking or sound the alarm by ringing the bell beside his bed that connected to a large network of chiming bells all over the castle. That, too, would betray him but would also bring a swift number of guards to his room in a matter of seconds. His only other option was escape through a hidden panel on the other side of his bed. He could leave unnoticed and unscathed, gather a group of soldiers once out of the escape route, and confront the knocking intruder unannounced from behind.

Before he could make a decision, the decision was made for him. The door—all that stood between him and this trespasser—was burning in a sudden, ferocious flame. Beon leapt over the bed, sword in hand, toward the hidden panel. He was through it in one fluid moment, making sure to close the panel quietly and quickly behind him. Running down the ramp and into the tunnels below the castle, he made decisions to preserve his people. He could've rung the alarm bells at any time, since the alarm system was strung through the tunnels as well, but now he knew he was dealing with the sorcerer. He did not want his guards and castle staff running toward the sorcerer without him and half his army alongside him.

He ran up a ramp hundreds of feet away from where he had run down, reached the hidden panel at the top of the ramp, and slid it open after unlocking the jig that kept it secured. It led him onto an empty street, darkened by midnight and the lack of gas streetlamps. He knew his way well, though, and ran straight to the General's quarters not far away. It was why he had chosen this ramp out of many possible exits from the secret tunnels.

Now it was his turn to knock in rapid fashion, hoping to wake up anyone in the home. He probably woke a few in other homes nearby, as he wasn't trying to be quiet. "General Morlay, get up. Now. It is the King. NOW!"

Beon heard stirring in the home—someone was up. The King saw the General look through a window at the disturber of his peace, while tying a sash around his robe. A few seconds later, the door was unbolted and opened, and the King stepped in as discreetly as possible considering his loud knocking and yelling just a few moments earlier.

"General, I believe the sorcerer is here. I awoke to loud knocking on my bedroom chamber, without a word being spoken to announce the intrusion. Before I could decide the best course of action, the door was aflame. I escaped through the tunnels and made my way here. I was not followed. I am sure of it."

"Did you sound the alarms?" the General's sleepy countenance just seconds ago had vanished into a look of pure terror.

"I thought of it but then thought better against it. I didn't want guards and others running toward my chamber to meet sorcerer. They would be imperiled. I decided my best bet was to leave and gather soldiers quickly and meet him from behind, surprised, if possible."

"Excellent, your majesty. Yes, I agree. I will gather three dozen that are still within the city and we will be ready in ten minutes. Stay here but look in my room to find as much as you can to arm and dress yourself for battle."

The King wondered how it was possible to dress for battle with flames of fire. He said nothing though and followed his General's direction to his back room to find whatever he could.

The General left through his home's side door. He lived in a section of the city that housed many soldiers. As he ran, he knocked on each door, yelling, as soldiers stumbled through doors drowsy and unalert. The General returned after several rounds, dressed in boots and gained his sword and shield as the King had found enough for both of them, and they were off, running quietly through the streets, soldiers falling in line behind them.

As they neared the front entrance to the castle, they were met by another group of sentries. "King!" The lead sentry bowed. "General!" He saluted. "We were on our way to alert you. An old lady reported seeing a large bird flying into the city not long ago. I determined it was odd enough to wake you with this news. I believe a large bird had been seen before the firebombing."

The General interrupted this report. "Very good. Join us. The enemy is here."

The sentry looked startled but said nothing, motioning the men and women behind him to follow along. Now they were four dozen. Four dozen against a man who could rule with fire.

Dayud waited for the door to burn. It was taking far too long. He'd heard nothing from the other side of the door since the first query of *Who's there?*

He looked over at Havorth—still in a trance, still not conscious. "Are you sure the King is in his chambers?" He demanded of the scribe.

Delirious from Dayud's power over him, Havorth swooned and droned, "He is always in his chambers at this time of night. Unless there is an emergency, of course."

Of course. The King might be staying elsewhere given that they had foreseen his river scheme. But there was no way the King could know that he, Dayud, would be here tonight. No one saw him. He was sure of it. Perhaps, Edora might have survived and made her way back to them?

No. Not possible. She had no transport. He had made his way straight away with transport. Even if she had found transport, he was sure he was the faster rider by far. They could not have anticipated the time or even the day of his arrival. They might just be on general alert and therefore moved the King as precaution. He had not thought of that. Where would the King go if he were not in his chambers? He had no insight. He could be anywhere. Was it the King who had queried him or a footman? There was no way to know until the door burned. He grew the flame to enhance the destruction of the thick wooden door.

In a matter of seconds, the door burned enough that Dayud stepped through the flame unharmed, leaving a still-dazed Havorth behind.

The King was not here. Clearly. But he had been. The bed showed definitive signs of having been slept in—covers were thrown open, sheets were rumpled, and if someone had danced on the bed, it would explain the random depressions on the duvet. The King had been here minutes ago.

Dayud yelled back to Havorth through the flaming door, the outer edges were still not burned through. "Where is the exit from this room, Havorth?"

"There is none, my love," Havorth drooled.

"There must be!" Dayud startled when he realized that the King might be hidden in the room somewhere, listening to the exchange, ready to strike him when he was least aware. He kicked under the bed in random places. Nothing. He set the dressers and cabinets on fire. Nothing. He pushed on bare walls. Nothing. He cast a spell, "Reveal the secrets." A wall panel he had pushed on rattled in place. It would not budge when he shoved it. He set it on fire, too. It would take a few minutes to burn and now the room was full of fire. It would not harm him at all, but it wasn't helping him fast enough. Stymied with fires of revenge burning the King's chambers and fires of rage burning inside his chest, he tried to think his way out. He turned suddenly to throw a flame when someone moved to his left. It was Havorth stepping through the now burned, flameless door.

"My love. Why is the room on fire? Where is the King?" Havorth monotoned as he looked wide-eyed and befuddled off into the far distance. Dayud was just about to throw him out, when everything changed.

Chapter Twenty-Three

The King led his soldiers. He wanted none of them at greater risk than he. What did he know of this sorcerer? Very little, except that he liked fire. What defeated fire? Water. When they reached the main gates of his castle, he directed the guards, "We are in extreme danger. Stay armed and ready to activate the water." Water pipes were installed in the halls and ceilings of nearly every room as fire extinguishers. He was grateful for them. "I will ring the alarm bells three times if you are to activate them."

The four guards nodded curtly, then saluted, allowing the King, the General, and his troops to enter. Three guards stayed on post, but one turned and went around the gate to a handle locked behind a small iron-barred window in the castle wall. The guard unlocked the window with a key on his key ring, opened the window and kept one hand on the handle, ready to unleash the water at any time. With his other hand, he unsheathed his sword and stood at the ready, as did one other guard. The other two guards pulled out their bows and strung arrows, ready to launch at a moment's notice.

The King led the soldiers through the halls quietly, carefully—signaling to non-essential staff along the way to seek safety, while guards in hallways were motioned to enlist with the attacking contingency. As they approached the King's chambers they slowed. The King's chambers could only be accessed through the maids' and butler's chamber. This servants' chamber had two entry doors. The maids' door connected to the kitchens. The butler's door led into one of the main hallways of the castle. With coded hand signals, General Morlay directed half the soldiers to circle around the halls with him to the maids' door. The King and the other half of soldiers headed directly to the butler's door. Both groups were both approaching blindly. They had no idea what they would find, if anything, when they entered the servants' chambers.

The King noticed heat as he neared the outer hall to the butler's door. He halted those behind him, grabbed the wire of the alarm system, and tugged three times.

In an instant, Dayud, Havorth, and the King's chambers were drenched in spraying water. The magicked fires were only slightly doused by the sprinklers set into the recesses of the ceiling. Dayud, on high alert, now knew that the King had escaped if only to release the water. Who he had with him, what his plans were, he did not know. Dayud realized he was cornered. He could firebomb his way out if needed. But he had no idea how many the King had alerted on his escape. He had no idea what they were armed with. He had no idea if he could make it out alive. He had intended to take the King hostage and bring Devor to its knees. He still could, but he needed to adapt.

Looking behind him, Dayud saw the secret panel was burned through enough to climb through. He grabbed Havorth and ran with him to the gaping hole. Dayud leapt through. The fire that still seared the wood, left him unscathed. But as he was pulling Havorth through behind him, Havorth screamed as his body burned from the flaming tongues lashing at him. Dayud kept pulling until Havorth was on the ground on the other side, still screaming in agony. Havorth rolled over and over, trying to extinguish the flames that moved over him like swarms of fire ants. The magick enchantments were difficult to overcome with the unmagicked element of dirt.

As Havorth lay writhing on the ground in pain that stabbed him from every direction, he looked up clear-eyed at Dayud. "What are you doing here? What's going on?" He was confused only to feel a scorching pain rise up out of his flesh morphing itself into another scream.

Havorth was no longer under Dayud's spell. The severe pain must have broken it, Dayud surmised. He needed a hostage, but Havorth, awake, conscious, and injured would only delay and hinder him. He turned and ran down the dirt ramp in the tunnels beneath the castle, leaving a thrashing Havorth behind.

Just outside the butler's entrance, the King heard someone shrieking—probably from pain—he thought, by the sharp wail of the scream. Whose voice it was, was undeterminable. Possibly male, though the shrieking was so high-pitched, even that was difficult to tell. Regardless, he suspected the sorcerer was near. Now was the time to act.

Water was still raining down on all of them. Beon barely noticed. He ordered his soldiers to follow him as he opened the butler's door to the servants' room. What he saw astounded him. Beon looked at the gaping, burned hole in the door to his chambers. Inside he could see much was on fire. The sprinklers were having some effect, but the flames lingered. Beon suspected normal water might be less than effective on bewitched fire. Looking around and not seeing the sorcerer, he motioned one of his soldiers to the other end of the servants' room, in order to open the opposite maid's door and let General Morlay and his troop in safely.

All fortysome were now crowded together in a room designed for a dozen at most. There was only one door into the King's chamber from the servants' room. General Morlay spoke with the King as discreetly as possible considering the cramped environs, "We need to attack quickly to gain the upper hand. Let's burst through this door, as many at a time as can fit."

King Beon considered his General's strategy. "No, let me go in alone. I don't want anyone else at risk until I can ascertain what's at stake."

General Morlay nodded at the King. So, Beon covered his face with a towel from the servants' cabinet that he'd moistened under the sprinklers. He stepped through the burnt door into his semi-burning room, following the sounds of screeches and moans. He could see his secret panel was almost burned through, too, and there was a body on the other side in the secret tunnel. Was it the sorcerer himself? Was it a trap? The King hesitated. What should he do?

Stepping back through the burned-out door, he said to the General, "There's a body through the secret panel in my room. I can't get close enough to see who it is. It could be the sorcerer, but we need to see if we can help."

189

General Morlay suggested, "Let's douse the room as much as possible. We can use the washing basins and containers from the kitchen and pour as much as we can on the flames."

"They seem to be resilient to water. Maybe magicked?" the King questioned.

"I concur," Morlay whispered, not wanting his soldiers to hear that he believed in anything like magicked fire, "but water is impacting them. Maybe more will get us close enough to get a good look at who it is on the other side of the panel."

The King agreed. They created a line from the kitchens to the bedroom and started filling basins, pots, tins, whatever they could find, and passing them down one to another all to the way to the King's chambers. The King insisted he be at the front of the line, dowsing the fires.

After numerous pourings of water on everything burning, the King could move closely enough to the panel to peer through it. The fires were odd. Water minimally impacted them, but neither did the fires spread. Why? What was the sorcerer's aim with burning and containing the burn? Wouldn't he want the fires to rage out of control? What was his larger purpose? King Beon had all of these questions blazing through his mind as he tossed every pail and pan, basin and tin of water. He peered through the door. "Hello? Who are you?"

Only moans and some small yips were coming from the obviously burned body. He couldn't make out the face. The victim had rolled over, so he was face down. At least Beon now knew it was a he. And he didn't look much like a sorcerer, dressed in mere bedclothes. The sorcerer was cunning, and a shapeshifter, though. The King had to be careful.

"Hello? Can I help you? Do you need help?"

The man, unable to talk, rolled himself partially.

King Beon gasped. "Havorth? Is that you?" Of course, it would be Havorth. The sorcerer knew how to use him, had used him. But where was the sorcerer? Hiding in the tunnels? He couldn't get out of them without burning his way through one of the five exit doors. They were all intricately locked and only the King and one caretaker—his trusted footman—had keys. Havorth was not the caretaker. Hardly anyone knew about the tunnels. The King was grieved that now, many Devorians would be aware there was more to the castle. His safe retreats were safe no more. This flashed through his mind in a second. Then, action.

"Morlay! It's Havorth. He's badly burned. Have some soldiers retrieve a stretcher in the medics room to carry Havorth back for treatment."

The General assented, "Sir!" Then he moved to the back of the room, taking two out of the water line and giving them orders.

"Hold on, Havorth. We're going to get you out of here and get you help," King Beon tried to extend any hope he could to his scribe.

While the King waited, he consulted with the General again. "The sorcerer is nowhere here. The tunnels are long, and he could be anywhere under the city. There are only five exits."

The General nodded. Most of this was news to him. He knew that, at times, the King had secret passage, but was ignorant as to where and what they were.

"The only way through each exit is a locked door and only I and one other have the keys. The sorcerer will not be able to get through unless he burns them like he did these. We are going to need more guards. Some stationed here. Some stationed at each of the five doors. He cannot escape. We are so close."

The General thought quickly. "The fires seem to be dying out on their own, so let's distribute guards now before he gets away."

"Agreed. Do it. The five exits are here." Finding some paper and a writing pen in the chamber room, the King drew a rough map of the city. The doors are here, here, here, here and here." He drew Xs on each hand-drawn door and then placed the numbers one through five beside them. "I will take some guards with me to this door, door number one. It's the farthest away and the closest to the walls and the gates. That's the tunnel I would take, if I were trying to escape. It's the longest one, though, and he likely does not know where he's going. I don't know what he knows. But I want to be close to the gates anyway in case he runs there."

"Doesn't he fly?" the General asked.

"True. I don't know how any of this works. We're just going to have to do the best we can, improvising as we go. Take ten guards for each door. Some with swords, some with arrows. We don't know what he's capable of. I'm leaving with ten now. Keep ten guards here too."

The King pointed and touched ten guards near him. He didn't have time for being selective about who was the most skilled. Now or never. "Let's go." And they ran out of the maid's chamber room, down the halls and out the main entrance of the castle. As he passed them, the King alerted the sentries of the castle to current strategies and sped to the far end of the city.

The General quickly divvied up the rest of the guards, keeping ten here, sending the other groups of ten each to a different door, running out with the count for the last door. Taking the last of the guards, they headed to the fifth door, as he knew it was near a sentry camp and he could round up more guards *en route*. "Make haste! Be ready for cunning and fire," he ordered each group. To the group staying, "Keep a few guards here at all times in case the intruder returns," he would not call him a sorcerer to his soldiers. "The rest of you, keep bringing water until these strange fires are dowsed completely."

Several minutes later, the King and his ten guards rounded a corner to a circle of houses. The secret door was hidden behind the houses in a shed that no one owned and no one paid any attention to. It was locked and looked undisturbed. The King knew all five doors would be guarded by now. Their door was the farthest away, by far. If something terrible had happened, one of the guards would have sounded an alarm horn. Each sentry had one. The horns were made from goats' horns and the sounded carried for miles. The kingdom-city was smaller than the reach of the horn's volume. Had the sorcerer already escaped? Doubtful. His only way through locked doors seemed to be through fire. Was he hiding in the tunnels waiting them out? Probable.

And then in a flash, the door in front of them burst into a bluish flame. The sorcerer was here! Now!

The King and his guards drew their swords and notched arrows on their bows, readying themselves for the moment they could attack through the burned door.

The sorcerer was furious. His strategy had been to use Havorth as a hostage when the King escaped. In negotiating for his release, he would light the King and his soldiers on fire, bringing Devor to its knees with him as conqueror. But now, he was running. He had no idea where he was, except that he could feel he was close to the northern border of the kingdom-city walls. This was the direction toward the volcanic fire, from which he drew his energy. He could always feel this magnetic power.

Once through this door, he would shapeshift and fly out to regroup and plan another attack that would not fail. He had not foreseen the escape of the King through an underground. Havorth hadn't informed him of it—probably because he had never known of it.

As he waited for the door to burn, he checked over his shoulder once, twice, again. He felt something stirring on the wind. What, he could not discern in his agitated state. He bent his mind and his will on avenging his family. This war was far from over.

The door now stood in flames with a small hole emerging at the foot. He waited for it to grow. He needed to wait to transform. His energy was still not at full measure since the battle with Edora. He need not risk his bird body in the flame unnecessarily.

He looked over his shoulder again. Were they behind him, following him up the tunnels? He needed to hurry. He decided to risk the transformation now. As a bird, he could just make it through the emerging hole in the door.

His skin darkened to jet black. His body shrank, his arms changed to wings, his legs thinned. His nose became beakish. It was enough. He was tired. He paused to gather his mind and then rushed through the hole.

The King and his soldiers gaped at the sight, stunned. A shiny bird so black it glinted blue in the dawning sun's light, emerged through the flaming hole at the foot of the door. It only took a moment, but the King found his mind. "Now!"

Arrows arched toward the bird. In a second, a bird's wing was caught, and in another second, the bird transformed into a man.

Dayud's eyes burned. He tore the arrow out of his now arm and cursed every arrow that sped towards him with flame, then boomeranged them back to their senders. He purposed a flaming arrow toward the King—only to miss.

The guards with swords dove at the sorcerer, slicing at him from every angle only to have flames thrown at them. Some dropped their swords, their hilts growing too hot to hold. More arrows torched as they flew. Another flame sped toward the King. He side-stepped it, ordering his guards to keep the arrows flying. Only one had to get through.

And then it happened. A flame hit a soldier, the King rushed to douse the flames by rolling him, and a flame hit the King, who rolled himself trying to dowse the angry magicked flames. He yelled orders to keep pursuing, but more of his soldiers went down, hit with flames.

Dayud had his opening. Escape or take the King hostage? In a split second, he decided to take the King. Putting a wall of flame around himself, he ran to the King, grabbed the arm that was still burning, pulled him through the wall of fire, and threatened them all in a voice that scalded, "If you do anything else to me, I'll kill the King. Here and now. Put down your weapons."
The King commanded, "Do not take orders from him. I am your King. Do what you have to do to bring him down…" but the King was hit with more flame and screamed.

More arrows flew, which burned in the wall of fire and went off course, missing the sorcerer.

"I warned you. He dies now!" Dayud yelled at them all.

The King was ready. Amidst his searing pain, he whispered, "My Niamá. Take me." In an instant, his body floated in a warm but not burning cloud. "If this is death, let it be." He closed his eyes, knowing he was safe. That it was over. That he had done everything he could to save his people and his great Devor.

Havorth writhed in his bed of torture, moaning. His nightmare was filled with whips of molten hot lashes on his arms and legs. Scorpions crawled over his body, attacking him with lethal stings. A bitter taste filled his mouth. If this was death, he wanted none of it. Life! Health! Freedom! He longed for it.

Chapter Twenty-Four

"Havorth, you are being treated in the royal medichè's room. You've just been given an herbal tonic to ease your pain. Can you hear me? My name is Maryah. I am your medic." She spoke to Havorth gently, not wanting to increase his suffering with loud words. After administering a tonic, she set down the syringe on a nearby tray, then washed her hands in a nearby basin and dried them. Havorth didn't respond except with more moans. In a few minutes he would sleep. Then she would dress his burns with healing salves. He could be saved—possibly. Did he have the will to live? To fight through the pain? That would remain to be seen.

"Madame Medichè, will Havorth live?"

The medichè turned to see one of the two soldiers who had brought him in entering the room.

"It remains to be seen."

"Will he be able to respond to questions soon?"

"He needs to sleep first. If he awakens, I'll determine his readiness then."

"If?" the soldier queried with a furrowed brow.

"If. He's burned on large parts of his limbs. His pain is quite severe. I've given him a tonic to put him to sleep below the consciousness of pain. If he lives through his injuries, and if he awakens to full consciousness, then I will determine his readiness. You may go." And she dismissed the soldier to his duty to guard the room by turning her back to him, listening to make sure he retreated as ordered.

The medichè watched Havorth's eye movements beneath his eyelids as they slowed. With her fingers, she felt the frantic pulse in his neck recede as he sunk gradually into a light unconsciousness. Then she began the arduous work of dressing his burns with healing salves. Never had she seen burns like these. He would need constant care for weeks if he lived. She almost felt it would be a mercy if he didn't.

Dayud watched as the King went from screaming to slumping. He was dead. He was sure of it. He let him drop to the ground. Now he could bring Devor to its knees. He turned to set more fire to any guards who remained. He could see through the fire wall that most of them were rolling on the ground trying to douse their magicked flames. He laughed to himself. He loved his power, his gift of fire. He looked at the others still standing, but they didn't move. They didn't raise an arm with a sword or a bow with an arrow. What were they doing?

It didn't matter. He would burn them all. He threw a flame at one of them. It stopped mid-air and fell to the ground. Dayud looked around and saw nothing. He threw another flame. Again, it stopped midway to his target and fell to the ground. He threw flame after flame but none of them reached their marks.

He looked down at the King, who was now outside the ring of fire. Dayud was startled by this but deduced that while throwing more flames, he had stepped closer to the soldiers and away from the King. The King was still. No surprise there. However, the flames on the King's body were also still. Dayud thought to himself, *Shouldn't the King be engulfed in flames?* Dayud gathered flame in his hand, gathered the fire in his entire body and he aimed at the King for another round of inferno to make sure he was good and dead.

He threw the ball of flame, his eyes eager to see the King engulfed in fire again. But the flame died out as soon as it left his hand. What was happening? Was he losing his power? Was he finally spent? He felt into his being and could feel the raging seas churning away. His fire power was still with him. So why was his magick dying?

He looked through the wall of fire and saw nothing and no one, save the remaining guards, still standing, still unmoving.

198

Edora felt her energy wane. She held her time shield around the King and around the soldiers, but she couldn't hold it forever. Soon it would give way and she would be forced to do battle with Dayud, putting the King and his guards at even more risk. She called forth all of her power. The time shield suspended them in the moment. They could not live, but they could not die either. Only Dayud could move, but his power was limited to his own time in which only he existed. She knew if he saw her, he could probably break the spell, but so far, he had not had the foresight to look up.

Upon arriving at the city gates, and being told Devor was on lockdown, she had implored the gateman to let her climb the outer wall. She may have used a little of her own magick to persuade him. She didn't regret it. And here she was on top of a city wall, looking down on the scene that she now held in the palms of her hands. The entire kingdom-city's outer walls were thick enough that two people could walk side-by-side around the top. The walkway itself had a waist-high parapet, so that if guards, who were the only ones who were ever walking there, needed to shield themselves, all they had to do was kneel down. Every several feet, a taller portion of stone that could shield the full height of a man was set into the outer side of the wall, along with an arrow slit, so archers could shoot any outside threat from a position of safety.

Being on the inside looking down, she had no place to hide. There were no waist-high—let alone—standing-high walls on the inside of the parapet walk. Devor's builders assumed the inside would be safe from hostile forces. If only they had known that in the future, the most hostile force Devor had ever faced was inside the walls. Edora was completely exposed.

Edora again felt her power drop. The guards who were burning when she suspended them in time, began burning again and rolling on the ground, and then stopping in mid-roll and starting again. She focused her power, especially around King Beon. She watched him, lying broken and burned, not knowing what state he was in. If only she could suspend his dying, maybe she could save him—if he weren't already gone. Dayud seemed confused watching the soldiers around him stop rolling and start and stop again. He threw flames, but still, they were fizzling out before they could reach their targets, moving or not.

Dayud spun around, keeping one eye on the King and the other on the soldiers. Most of the soldiers were in some state of suspended or active burning. The rest remained unharmed but moved only sporadically. He didn't know who was controlling his magick, but he intended to destroy them. He searched relentlessly through his fire wall.

Edora knew Dayud would look up eventually. She needed to keep him distracted as long as she could. Every moment was another moment of salvation.

General Morlay had arrived at the fifth door with as many guards as he could round up—eight. He knew that since several minutes had passed, either the sorcerer would be at one of the doors or still hiding in the tunnels. He had a decision to make. He could wait here, doing nothing, or he could act. He acted. He was a man of action. He ordered five of the soldiers with him to stay and stand guard and to blow their horns if the sorcerer appeared.

Still having the King's hastily drawn map of the other doors with him, he took the three remaining guards, intending to go door-to-door to see if the sorcerer had appeared at any of them. Arriving at door four, he saw ten guards doing exactly what he'd ordered them to do, all eyes on the door with bows and swords readied for action. "Four of you—stay here and stand guard. The rest—you are with me."

They gathered the six with their three and made their way to the third door. They encountered the same again. Ten guards ready. Nothing else happening. He again ordered four to stay. The rest were with him.

Onto the second door, they found ten guards, but no action. He left the same as before and took up his gathering troops to head to the first door. He now had twenty-one with him.

After consulting the map one last time, General Morlay—with his own soldiers right behind him—ran to the first door, where the King had gone with ten guards. Nearing the target door, they rounded a circle of homes. In front of them, Morlay saw the sorcerer throwing flames. The General was glad for the extra bodies, bows, and horns. "Battle! Shoot! Blow!"

In an instant, arrows started flying toward the sorcerer. Horns started blowing into the early morning air, the melancholic moans flying even faster toward the ears of those who would hear and help.

Another moment later, General Morlay watched all of the arrows drop in front of the sorcerer like an invisible wall surrounded him, saw several soldiers on the ground burning and some suspended in motion. And the King—the King!—lay on the ground with flames on different parts of his body—but the flames were frozen, like red ice. Dead or alive? he didn't know. What he observed was beyond his ability to understand.

He saw a movement and looked. Up. There was the lady-in-white, Edora, holding out her hands. Was she helping them or helping the sorcerer? He didn't know.

He looked back down to see the sorcerer had followed his gaze to the top of the city wall.

Edora! How? How could she be alive, let alone here? Now? What power animated her? Dayud had no idea, but the rage that had smoldered in him since he was a child, since his family was outcast from their city, was now burning like a wildfire in a forest after years of drought. Edora's mother had cursed his brother, and he had died. In seeking revenge on them for their evil curse, Dayud's father commissioned men to slay them all. The father was found and captured. After interrogating him, he revealed where his wife and daughter had gone, and the men revenge-murdered him with a single sword strike through his stomach. But they found he lied. The mother and Edora were not where the father said they were and were nowhere to be found. They had escaped.

Dayud's father's actions had stirred a village revolt against his family. They too had been bewitched by Edora's mother and lived in the sway of her vast, persuasive powers. Not wanting more evil to befall them for her exile and the father's murder, they demanded that the King exile Dayud's father from the kingdom. They stopped working their fields, standing outside the castle day after day until the King relented. It was a relatively simple transaction for the King. He was threatened by Dayud's father's wealth and his standing. Dayud's father was great and therefore a danger to the King. And so, the King threw him out, along with his family. They wandered for days, hungry, starving until they found a village, far away from the King's influence, that took them in. It was there that Dayud found his teacher, the master sorcerer, who took him under his tutelage and flamed the burning embers of revenge.

This all passed through Dayud's mind in an instant. Now he could have his ultimate revenge on Edora and the kingdom-city that protected her. He would have the power his father should have had, both in influence and wealth, with the added measure of sorcery for protection. He would finally avenge his father's honor.

Dayud strengthened the line of fire between himself and the King's guards, adding more intensity and heat. Then, he ignited flame in his hands and aimed it at Edora. He could see her looking straight at him, whispering words of enchantment. He threw the fireball at her. He knew Edora's waterpower would protect her, but the threat would interrupt her focus and then he could finally defeat them all.

Upon seeing more of the King's soldiers arrive and Dayud notice her on top of the wall, Edora prepared for a fire attack. Now she could use water to fight his sorcery. If she'd used her waterwitching before, Dayud would have discovered her. But instead of a fire attack on her, Dayud first turned and put more fire between him and the newly arrived guards.

Edora waited for the perfect moment. She watched Dayud turn back and look at her again, magicking fire in his hands. As he aimed his fireball at her—his attention solely on her—Edora magicked a waterfall behind Dayud's back. His wall of fire disappeared in plumes of steam. Now the newly arrived troops had their chance. As Dayud's fireball drew closer to her, she dissolved it in water and watched.

General Morlay went stone-cold inside. The battle he and his guards had stumbled onto would haunt his dreams for years to come. Fire and water were chasing each other, seemingly alive and fighting, and time was starting and stopping. He assessed his options quickly, but how could he counter the manipulation of elements and even time itself?

Then, suddenly, a barrage of water hit the fire line between his soldiers and the sorcerer. "Attack!" he yelled.

Pain shot through Dayud like he had never felt before. More and more pain, penetrating his every cell. He cursed and looked down at his body to see what had happened.

Stunned, Dayud saw arrows and swords sticking into him in multiple places. "Edora!" he screamed. It was his last conscious action.

General Morlay watched the sorcerer fall, full of slings and arrows. His guards had slain the sorcerer. He and Devor's soldiers cheered.

With Dayud lying still on the ground, Edora breathed in, trying to restore her power. The guards Edora had put a time shield around to save them from burning to death, screamed in pain. Her time shields had fallen. She attempted her time shields again. They didn't work. King Beon was burning again, too. Her power was nearly gone. If the King was still alive, she needed to get her time shield up around him immediately. If he was still alive. If he could even be saved. But the time shield would not take. In desperation, she magicked water into her hands, and mimicking Dayud, threw water balls at the King and his soldiers to try to douse the fires. It had minimal impact, barely shrinking the magicked flames.

She noticed water running down her face and didn't even realize she had been crying. She couldn't lose King Beon now. Not after all this. Not after everything that had happened. He had to live. He had to. Her heart broke open. She fell on her knees and sobbed ib torrents; her powers run dry.

The triumphant, ringing cheer that went up didn't last long as they all noticed the King and several of his guards start burning in flames. It was unreal and all too much for General Morlay to make sense of quickly. He ordered his guards, "Try to smother the fire with coats, shirts, dirt, anything you can find!"

He himself ran to the King, but the hot flames kept him from getting too close. Shedding his coat, he whacked at the fire on the King, attempting to get it to die down enough to approach and smother it. It was no use. He looked around and his guards were also having no luck putting out the other fires. He raised his eyes to the lady-in-white, but she was collapsed on her knees at the top of the wall, weeping. Was the King lost?

"Save the King!" he yelled. Several of the guards ran to the General's side and tried smothering the fire with their cloaks as well. Nothing was working.

In the chaos, General Morlay feeling helpless looked up at Edora, "Lady-in-White! Can't you do something to save the King?"

Edora looked at him and put out her hands. Nothing happened. She shook her head, then put her head in her hands again, still weeping.

General Morlay was not going to give up so easily. "Get water. Now!" he commanded his guards. By now, many Devorians had gathered around the scene. Faces in shock, faces in tears, faces pinched in fear.

His guards started looking around for water. Morlay intervened. He yelled to the Devorians: "We need water. Who has water who lives close by?"

A few Devorians raised their hands. "Follow them!" he ordered the guards.

Flames still ravaged the King's body and a few of his guards. Water wasn't going to make it in time.

Chapter Twenty-five

After seeing the large bird fly in and reporting it to soldiers, the old lady—a widow named Livya—slowly followed the action. One careful step with a cane after another, she now came upon a terrible scene.

The King and several soldiers were burning. Cloaks being slung at the flames were not smothering them. She looked down and saw one man lying dead, full of arrows and swords, looking like a giant pin cushion. She looked up and saw a woman in white kneeling on the city wall, crying. Was it *the* lady-in-white? She'd thought she was a myth, a rumor, a bit of city gossip stirred up by jealous women who fantasized that they should be the next queen of Devor.

Across from her, a small man hobbled up to the scene. No one was paying any attention to him, though she noticed him immediately, perceptive as she was. He looked at her, gave a little nod, a slight bow. Then raising his hands, she watched the impossible happen. The fires all went out in exploding poofs. The King who had been lying perfectly still, started moaning and rolling around. The soldiers who had just moments ago been burning alive, writhing in pain, were now quiet, seemingly resting peacefully.

With another wave of a hand, the King, too, stopped his sudden motions and moans, and seemed to be peacefully asleep.

The old woman saw everyone take in the instant changes. The lady-in-white stood up and cheered, jumping up and down. The General of the soldiers ran to the King, feeling for a pulse, and indicated a yes with a nod and a loud, "He's alive!" The General ran to each of his guards who'd been burning. All were alive. He started taking charge, "Get the King and all of these guards to the medichè. Now!"

The old man stayed in the background, even hiding behind Devorians. He caught her gaze, looked back at her, and held a single finger up to his lips. She nodded back her agreement to keep quiet. *Who was he?* she thought to herself. She intended to find out.

Edora, beside herself with joy, now knew the King was alive. Sensing a sudden change, she had looked down and through bleary tears had seen the fires magicked away and signs of life in Beon. She knew who had done it too. She searched the growing crowd as the sun rose in the early morning sky. Where was he? He had made it in good time, much better than she anticipated. Finally, seeing the top of his balding head as he tried to stay undiscovered in the still-gathering crowd, she ran back along the top of the wall, to the stairs down near the gate. She ran to where she had last seen Jaxper, but he was gone. Where did he go? She raced around looking for him, but he was nowhere to be seen.

Knowing he would show up eventually, she ran to the soldiers who were carrying the King off to the medichè. She followed hoping some power might return to her to be of some use in the King's mending.

Jaxper made himself as invisible as he could. There was still danger. The General had made it the priority to get the King and his guards some healing help and had carried them all away. The body of the sorcerer, Dayud, laid on the ground, forgotten. Jaxper kept his eye on the body, even as he weaved and wove between the onlookers. Many were now dispersing. Likely, some went back to their homes, their work, or followed their King to the castle for news, for respect, for prayers to the Devorah—the mother spirits of Devor Edora had told him about on her first visit to Javenia.

As he saw Edora leave for the castle, too, he breathed a sigh of relief. She had done what she had to do. He wanted her in no more danger. She had played her part very well. But there was more he had kept from her. There had been no way to teach her everything he knew in such a short amount of time. She was a natural. She excelled, but she was still naïve in the ways of dark magick.

Jaxper was finding fewer people to hide behind, though no one was paying him much attention anyway. He occasionally caught sight of an older woman who had espied his magick and was continuing to keep an eye on him. He didn't want her to come any closer.

An hour later, there were still Devorians walking by, hovering, looking at Dayud's body and the scene of the firefight.

Jaxper watched over it all. He was well aware Dayud was not dead.

Edora followed the General and his soldiers closely. She couldn't yet feel her power returning, but she wanted to be in the King's presence in case it did.

At the castle door, she made her way to follow the rescue party inside, but was stopped by a guard, who clearly thought her a commoner.

"No. I must go in. I live here."

"Only the King lives here. The rest are servants."

"Yes, yes, I am a servant. I live up there." And she pointed behind them, to her tower.

The guard turned and looked at her. "By order of the General, none get in that are not given his permission."

Astounded, she started yelling ahead. "General! General! General Morlay! Please let me in. I must come in. Please!"

There was no indication that any of the soldiers were paying her any attention, and she had no idea if the General could even hear her from this far back. Her anger boiled over and she felt her powers rise up just enough. "I will have entrance," she ordered the guard and with a dismissive shift, he let her pass.

Quietly, she glided through the halls behind the guards. She didn't know where they were taking the King, but she needed to be there.

She knew it in her bones. She had to be there. Her heart and soul demanded it. Finally, they came to a winding stair up one floor. She again followed behind and as the door ahead was about to close, she called for the General, "Please, General! I can help the King."

Of course, she couldn't guarantee any outcome. Still, she needed to be there. Somehow, the King's life still depended on her.

General Morlay appeared at the door. He knew who she was, the lady-in-white. He had watched her display her powers. She was obviously not all-powerful. Her powers had flickered, waned, and then out of nowhere, everything was saved. He wasn't sure how it had all finished so well, when she had seemed so defeated.

He understood a little more why the King might want her around. She was no danger to the King, that much he knew. She was dangerous, though. She was not someone to be trifled with. How had she gotten into Devor and then the castle, for instance, when they were both on lock-down? Did she have her own secret entrance?

He assessed all of this in a few seconds. She was here to protect the King. That was enough for now. He let her enter.

The old woman, Livya, kept an eye on the little bald man who had indicated that she stay quiet. Strange things were afoot, and she was not going to let anything get by her that could endanger her family or Devor.

Most of the onlookers had moved along. Nothing to see anymore. She wondered why the General hadn't taken the arrowed body away or at least left a guard or two. Did he not care? Maybe not. Did he forget? Maybe. With all the chaos and crisis of the moment and the need to get the King and the guards cared for as quickly as possible, perhaps he'd simply let it slip his mind.

Who had this body been? she wondered. Dressed all in black, with a black cloak, he looked as ominous as an approaching dark storm cloud in the middle of the day. He was out of place in every way. Even if he'd been in street clothes, people would have noticed him.

The old bald man was clearly not Devorian, either. His skin was lighter than the average Devorian. Much lighter. He was dressed head-to-foot in colorful, wrapped cloaks. He was even barefoot. However, despite his oddity and the plumage of his cloaks, no one seemed to notice him, except for her. How he could be so colorful and yet nearly invisible to everyone else, vexed her.

As people continued to drift by, she saw the old man disappear behind a cottage. She moved her position so as to see him, but when she was in place, he was not where she'd expected him to be. She moved back to her original place, to see if he had gone around the cottage, but no, he was not there either. She started, then, to walk toward the cottage. Looking behind other homes, sheds, and shrubs, she couldn't find him anywhere.

Knowing she'd been given the slip, she went back to watch the body. Somebody had to.

Jaxper watched the old lady watching him. Now was the time to make his move. Most of the passersby had moved on. Seemingly dead bodies were boring after a while. Most of the remaining crowd moved in the direction of the castle, presumably to catch wind of the condition of their King.

He ducked behind the cottage, and then he magicked himself away—only to reappear behind another cottage on the opposite side of Dayud. No one could see him here. He watched as Dayud's energy continued to drift above his body. Dayud's magick was strong enough to restore his body back to health—strong enough to enter someone else's body—strong enough to haunt the King, torturing the Kind's mind into chaos. To do so, though, Jaxper knew Dayud needed to keep his body from further decline, in stasis.

Dayud's energy was attached to his dying body. All Jaxper needed to do was to make sure his body didn't live, or make sure his energy and the body would separate completely.

Jaxper decided the former would be easier. Dayud's body was closer to death and dying every moment, even as Dayud's soul was gathering its strength to focus his powers to do whatever he decided to do to continue his life one way or the other.

Jaxper magicked his own fire in his hands. It was something he had kept from Edora. Something he had hidden for her own sake. He knew fire, he was a master of fire, because he had learned from the same teacher that Dayud had.

Jaxper threw a fireball at Dayud's body. The body caught flame and burned. Jaxper watched as Dayud's energy looked around for the source of the flame. He disappeared himself again, reappearing behind different cottages, to keep Dayud from focusing in on him. In Dayud's energy state, he had the power to see Jaxper even behind walls. But Jaxper knew that by changing positions frequently, it would be difficult for Dayud to discover him until it was too late.

Jaxper peeked around the cottage he was currently behind and watched Dayud's body continuing to burn. Soon, it would be over for good. He saw the old woman step closer to the body.

"NO!" Jaxper yelled.

Dayud hovered above his body, watching the King and his burned guards carried off to the castle, his own body dying, stuck with swords and arrows. How could this have happened? He saw Edora running off too, but she looked weak. She could not have executed the magick that had been performed after he succumbed. Looking around for the source of the magick, he caught glimpses of a strong magick but couldn't focus. His body was weakening and with it, his connection to his body. He needed to focus, stay attached. With focus he could rejuvenate his body enough to stay alive until some energy returned to it, enough to transform, enough to heal.

He felt himself floating higher away from his body. Then, in an instant, his body caught flame—magicked—it appeared to him, and his focus blurred even more.

Using the very last minutiae of his own magick, he powered himself closer to his body. He couldn't put the fire out with his dwindling energy. That was clear. His energy looked around and glimpsed a familiar face. Jaxper? It couldn't be. He was here? How? Why?

And then an old woman drew closer. His only hope. As he took over her body, he heard Jaxper yell and her scream.

Jaxper raced forward, not caring who saw him, if anyone. He threw a flash of light at the old woman's body. If anyone caught sight of it, it probably looked like he was throwing a lightning bolt at her. He chuckled, even as his serious nature took over. The woman convulsed.

He threw another bolt of light. She convulsed again.

Did he risk another bolt? Any more might kill her, but with Dayud's energy within her, Dayud could do any number of magick feats to escape in her body and her life would be over anyway.

Jaxper waited. He started to see her body transform. He threw another bolt. Her body convulsed, she rolled over and vomited.

Dayud's soul was thrown from her body. Jaxper threw a bolt at Dayud's own burning body, just in case Dayud tried to re-enter and salvage whatever was left of it. With it he added an incantation to undo the hex, the curse Dayud had laid on Jaxper's family. This was the final piece that was needed in order to dissolve the destructive energies from the Stallexi family, so they could never attack Edora again. Jaxper waited and watched. Dayud's energy dissipated, dissolved into the ether. It was over. Finally, the nightmare that had begun with his and Edora's family's long exile was finished.

He went to the old woman who was lying still on the ground beside Dayud's now deceased remains. He felt for a pulse. She'd survived. He hexed her with a sleeping spell and left. She would be fine, but she might have some mighty strange dreams while she slept. He chuckled again to himself.

Looking around and seeing that no one was watching, he left. His work in Devor was done. He would catch up with Edora soon enough, when all was well.

King Beon opened his eyes, trying to stretch his limbs, to feel into his flesh and bones. Was he alive after all? He must be. What had felt as light as air to him, now felt heavy, earth-bound. The forces of gravity he had always taken for granted, now seemed like a punitive blanket, keeping his trapped soul from flying.

He could see bandages over his hands and feet. What had happened? His memory hazy, he tried to speak, to ask for help in remembering. But all that happened in his dry throat was a crack of vocalization.

It was enough.

The lady-in-white appeared at his bedside. *Edora, that's her name,* he thought, shaking his head slightly, trying to dislodge the fuzzy thoughts that wouldn't sharpen, wouldn't clear enough for him to think.

"King Beon, I'm so glad to see your eyes. You have been asleep for many hours. How are you feeling?" Edora asked him.

"What happened?" he asked her, though he knew his words were muddled by his thick tongue and parched vocal folds. Would she understand him?

Resting her hand gently on the King's wrapped left hand, she looked him directly in the eyes. "We are safe. We are all safe. You and your soldiers battled Dayud, the great sorcerer. He is dead now. You and some others were burned, but you're all going to be okay. Havorth, too. You're in the medich. Salves and ointments will help your skin heal, and the medichè has given you herbs to help relieve the pain. Are you in pain?"

He shook his head. "Water?"

She nodded and left his side to return with a large syringe full of water. "Just a few sips at a time. The herbs will make you extra thirsty, but we need to let them have their full effect for cutting the pain, so just a bit of water whenever you need it."

She placed the syringe gently between his lips, and slowly squeezed the sheepskin-dried bulb at the top of the hollowed-out sheep bone. Liquid flowed into his mouth. Swallowing hurt. But the water relieved much of his dry throat, so he didn't care. He was glad she was near. He felt his heart stir. Relieved Edora hadn't been a casualty of the sorcerer's treachery, he thirstily drank everything within the syringe, and then felt himself drifting back to sleep.

When the King closed his eyes, Edora again placed her hands over the King's wounds, hovering over the burns, sending them energy. As she did, she felt her own energies continue to gain strength, and she channeled everything she could to heal his skin.

Chapter Twenty-Six

6 MONTHS LATER

Ædora sat, bewitching the waters. Her hands hovered over the scrying bowl as she chanted and lowered her eyes to shut out the distracting and noisy public scenes that surrounded her in her tower.

As she felt herself slip into that easy space between waking and sleeping, where all was possible to see, she leaned over the scrying waters and opened her eyes.

The waters foamed, rolling and spinning, never forming anything but movement. She waited patiently, to see what the waters would foretell.

They refused.

Before the cock crowed on that cold, dark morning, King Beon was up, stretching and walking, still getting used to sensing his healed skin pulled taut by the burns and healing salves. He was feeling more like himself every day. Today, though, was the day. He had asked his Niamá, if she still could hear him, to provide a shield around his thoughts and activities. He needed the secrecy. No one could know what he was about to do.

Havorth was asleep when he heard knocking at his door. He tried to ignore it, rolling over and trusting the early riser would go away if ignored.

Whoever they were, they did not. The knocking was louder the second time. And truly deafening the third time.

"Alright, alright. I'm coming," Havorth snorted out his words as he rolled out of bed, slipped into his house shoes and grabbed his nightcoat off the bedpost on his way to the door, as slowly, as measured, as his recovering body could take him.

Opening it, Havorth was stunned to see the King standing at his door.

"Why didn't you say it was you! I would've come right away, my liege!" Havorth replied disdainfully yet with an apologetic tone as he bowed painfully, with a twinging face.

The King entered and closed the door behind him. "I don't want anyone to know I'm here," he said, looking around as if there might be people hiding in Havorth's one-room cottage. "Can you keep a secret?"

Havorth flushed. Of course he could, but was this some type of test to embarrass him because of the scandal of the sorcerer? What was the King up to?

"Eh, I…"

Before he could answer, the King continued, "I need you to open the doors to the stairway to Edora's tower, then remove the guards, so they can't see that I'm the one entering. Only you can do this."

Yes, yes, only he could do this. He had recently been reassigned as the key and riddle maker for the secret tower. Now that the sorcerer—his former lover—was dead, and the inquiry into the sorcerer's first excursion into the castle had been found to be due to sorcery and not Havorth's treachery, he had his old job back. Well, one of them. He still was not the scribe. His hands had been burned badly, and though he was slowly getting back his ability to write, it would take time to learn to do so quickly enough to be the royal scribe again. His hands ached if he went too fast. So, for the time being, he was the royal key and riddle maker. Ah well. At least he had a job again and wasn't bored out of his mind imprisoned in his own home with nothing to do.

"Of course, my King. Let me tidy myself, and we'll be off. At once, you mean, yes?"

"Yes, as soon and as quickly as you can ready yourself. Thank you."

Havorth retired to the privacy of his washroom, muttering to himself, "What does the King want with the lady-in-white at this time in the morning? Can't be good. Why am I the one who has to do this menial job? I'm worth so much more than this drivel." Now that all of Devor knew about the King's underground tunnels, they had had to be filled in. They were more of a danger than a protection, as anyone could gain secret access to the castle. The King thus had no private entrance to Edora anymore and so, again, Havorth became the escort.

Brushing aside his own comments as he also brushed aside the few strands of hair that had awkwardly placed themselves in his sleep, he turned and approached King Beon. "Ah, ready to go, my liege. Anything for you," he bowed and put on a cheerful face although inside he was anything but.

At the tower, while the King hid behind a corner, Havorth unlocked the doors that were his to unlock, spoke the answers to the riddles at the appropriate doors with guards and then ordered them both down to the broom closet.

The guards protested up a storm, but Havorth insisted or they'd be released from duty, and they finally relented.

Then he allowed the King up, while locking all the bottom doors behind him and letting the guards out of the broom closet. "Stay here and guard the first door. When you hear knocking from the other side of the first door, one of you stay here, and one of you come and get me. You'll return to the broom closet when I get back, then I'll let the visitor out, and you can return to your regular posts. Any questions?"

The guards shook their heads and stood at attention in front of the first door.

Havorth shook his head at the frivolous rules for the lady-in-white and went back to his cottage in the castle. He was going to sleep again if he could, until the King was ready to leave.

Before the King made it up the stairs, he was breathing heavily. He knew he needed to get back into shape after his convalescence. He stopped and rested until he regained some semblance of normal respiration. Then, rather than going up to the top door, he took the hidden side door that led directly into Edora's apartment. Only he could access this route. The hidden tunnels were gone and their private access to Edora's tower, but this secret access remained. He didn't want to scare Edora or interrupt anything private, but this was the way it must be done.

As he came through the door into her apartment, he looked down in case he had, in fact, interrupted her in privacy, and paused, calling out to her, "Edora! It's Beon. May I enter?"

Edora sat right in front of the door, poised over her scrying waters, with her mouth wide open as she noticed the King—her King Beon—now framed by the secret doorway. "Yes?" she answered tentatively, not sure what was happening, since the waters had not been forthcoming with any secrets. She would soon find out why.

Beon looked up and upon seeing her sitting there, he strode forward, trying to hide what was left of his exhaustion. He knelt in front of her, held out a delicately carved ring of precious metals, and spoke softly, "Edora. I have loved you for a long, long time. I know that now, after everything that has happened over the past several months. And now it is time. Will you?"

The End

To Be Continued...

Book Totem: Horse

On Native American traditions, Horse represents power. Horsepower is an earthly ability and a spiritual ability, enabling humanity to "fly" on land and shamans to "fly" in spirit. Horsepower represents the wisdom to balance all elements: fire and water, earth and sky, so that power is not distorted.

The Akhal-Teke breed pictured here—called the "sacred horses" by the Russians and sometimes referred to as the "golden horses" because of their unique metallic sheen—are known for their speed, toughness, endurance, and intelligence. This was the first horse to carry Edora on her journey.

Acknowledgements

I am filled with awe and gratitude for all who helped propel this book into publication.

Thank you especially to

Cathy, Kim, and Marianne, for your editing, comments, and support of my craft over many years.

My loving family for tolerating my love of all things mystical, magical, other-worldly, no matter how fantastical.

My friends, clients, students, and readers, for continuing to walk this journey with me in myriads of heart-centered ways.

Lindsay Trini of LT Arts for the fabulous cover design.

The Light—the muse that descended into my mortal plane—to grant me this fiction plot. This was the first of many plots that have been downloaded to me during sleep. I hope I have done this gift justice, helping it rise to its best potential.

Many blessings and much Love and Light to you all.

Monica McDowell
July 2020

About the Author

$\mathcal{A}$ healer by day and a writer by night, Monica McDowell is a certified Karuna® Reiki Master who has spent countless hours meditating on the virtues of chai lattes and chocolate. She was born and grew up in the Pacific Northwest, by the banks of the Nooksack River waters, in the land of the Nooksack peoples, near the waters of the Salish Sea. She lives with her husband by the waters of the Large Lake in Seattle, Washington, home of Chief Sealth of the Lushootseed peoples, in the shadow of Mt. Tahoma, mother of all waters.

Connect with Monica

Email: monica@monicamcdowell.com
Website: www.monicamcdowell.com
Facebook: facebook.com/monica.mcdowell or /revmonicamcdowell
Twitter: twitter.com/monicamcdowell

Monica McDowell has the distinction of being the first ordained minister in the USA granted civil rights by a federal ruling. She received her Master of Divinity degree from Princeton Theological Seminary in spiritual care and counseling and graduated summa cum laude as co-valedictorian from Seattle Pacific University

Made in the USA
Monee, IL
05 August 2020